Birds

Volume One

NCPA ANTHOLOGY

A collection of fiction and nonfiction animal stories
by NCPA authors and poets.

ELVA ANSON, EVERETT ANSON, DEV BERGER,
JULIE BEYERS, DENISE LEE BRANCO, T.A.
BRANDON, A.K. BUCKROTH, PATRICIA E.
CANTERBURY, RACHEL CHU, SHARON S DARROW,
ROBERTA L. DAVIS, KIMBERLY A. EDWARDS,
ELAINE FABER, LAURA GARFINKEL, JAN HAAG,
M.L. HAMILTON, BOB IRELAN, ANGELICA
JACKSON, CHARLENE JOHNSON, DUNCAN
MACVEAN, D.V.M., L.D. MARKHAM, KATHY LYNNE
MARSHALL, DEBORAH MELTVEDT, MATTHIAS
MENDEZONA, NANCY J. MILLER, ELLEN OSBORN,
STEVE PASTIS, CAROLYN RADMANOVICH,
DOROTHY RICE, AMY ROGERS, NORMA JEAN
THORNTON, JUDITH VAUGHAN, CHRISTINE L.
VILLA, DÄNNA WILBERG, BARBARA YOUNG

BIRDS OF A FEATHER: Volume One

A collection of fiction and nonfiction animal stories by NCPA writers and poets.

Published by
Samati Press
P.O. Box 214673
Sacramento, CA 95821
www.sharonsdarrow.com

This book is independently published by Samati Press in arrangement with individual members of Northern California Publishers & Authors: www.norcalpa.org.

Printed in the United States of America

ISBN: 978-1-949125-05-4 (paperback)
      978-1-949125-06-1 (ebook)

Table of Contents

WILD REGRET

LAURA GARFINKEL

Baby owl, where did you come from?

Did you Come From Away like
an errant pilot, crash landing in
foreign territory—falling from the sky?

Or perhaps you had a home in a nest
high above this yard atop the Silver Maple
in the air above the property lines
and in the skies which no one
has a right to own.

Your wildness startled me on that Sunday
in the middle of my domesticity.
My thought was to protect your wounded
body from the little white dog who lives inside,
or perhaps, to protect her from you.

You lay crumpled and helpless as I loomed above you
meeting your gaze. One wing flapped
weakly as you lay barely moving.

Mortally wounded and suffering, I assessed.
End-of-life, I judged.
Have courage, I decided.
Rise to this unfortunate challenge, I thought.

I summoned my preoccupied husband
to bring the shovel, gloves, and black bags.

Afterwards I walked alone
along the river parkway. I thought
of how we had traded places and how
I walked among the trees that had belonged to you.
The earlier events played backwards in my mind.
As the morning progressed, so did my regret
and then my doubt and guilt and shame.
I wrestled with what might have been
and what I wish was, instead.

There, gently scooping feathered baby into
a box lined with newspaper and rags
to bring to the nature preserve we
visited so often when young children
with their own wildness nested at home.

We used to walk the trails there, and
visit the rescued and rehabilitated animals
saved and housed in their recreated habitats inside.

Would my reaction of mercy killing
have been more an instinct of life-saving if
I'd had those little ones of my own as witness guides?
And would you have chosen to trade your wildness for
a life behind glass—captured and caged?

Laura Garfinkel is an "aspiring" poet as well
as a longtime and "accomplished" mother
and wife. She works as a Medical Social
Worker and lives in Sacramento. She is part
of a wonderful Tuesday night writing group.

BALTHAZAR, THE MALLARD AND OTHER STORIES

STEVE PASTIS

"Always play your cards close to your feathers," said Balthazar the Mallard. "And always leave with at least one chicken joke untold."

With those pearls having been shared, Balthazar the Mallard took flight south. The foxes, deer, antelopes, and bees were sorry to see him go, but autumn was almost over and they all had to prepare for the coming winter. It was expected to be an especially cold and unpleasant one and they all had things to do. Some had shopping, some had knitting, and others needed to repair their roofs, hives, or nests.

The winter was even worse than predicted, but this led them to celebrate springtime with extra fervor. They held a spring festival and had plenty of food and wine. They even hired a DJ.

Between the dinner and the dancing, Balthazar the Mallard once again flew into their midst and took the stage.

"Keep your eyes on the approaching headlights," said Balthazar the Mallard.

"Why don't you stuff your silly bill full of feathers?" shouted one of the deer.

Balthazar the Mallard was startled. When the foxes, deer, antelopes, and bees broke into applause, he was stunned.

"You hung onto my every word in the fall? And now, in the spring you want me to stuff my bill with feathers? What gives?"

"In the fall, you were our last diversion before having to prepare for a tough winter," said the deer who had made the feathers comment. "Now in the spring, you are keeping us from having fun."

With that the DJ started spinning his first record, a funky tune by Wild Cherry. The animals took to the dance floor as Balthazar the Mallard flew away.

Sometimes it's a good thing to know why others like you.

KEYS TO THE PLANET BOOTH

Ned lamented that the keys to his planet booth were buried in the snowy mess that had once been a happy azalea bed.

"It's not supposed to snow here," he said as he looked through his picture window at the snowy mess. "It's not fair and they promised it wouldn't snow."

"It's your own darn fault for leaving the keys by what was once our happy azalea bed," noted his wife, Angora. "What were you thinking, Ned? You could have left your planet booth keys in the butter dish by our three-platter toaster and you would be a much happier camper at the present time."

The doorbell interrupted Ned's mental search for a response. He opened the door to see three penguins on his front porch.

"We'd like to see your planet booth," said the penguin in the floppy bonnet. "We'd like the whole tour and some overpriced souvenirs also."

"Sorry, but the planet booth is locked," apologized Ned. "The keys are buried in a snowy mess that was once our happy azalea bed."

"Maybe we can help," responded the only penguin to speak in this story. "We are happy to search through snowy messes. In fact, we like them."

Angora, who was now standing beside her husband, nudged him with her knuckles.

"Oh, that's right," said Ned. "That wouldn't be a good idea. We laid penguin traps all around what had been our happy azalea bed to keep out pesky penguins. Now that we could use help from you penguins, this sort of works against our current aspirations. Does this qualify as irony, or what?"

Ned and the only penguin who speaks in this story deliberated the meaning of irony and found it missed the mark in this situation.

The penguins left. Angora was going to build on her previous criticism of Ned when the doorbell rang again. This time, it was an elk.

"I'd like to see the planet booth," said the elk. "I may even offer a corporate sponsorship if I am pleased with it."

Ned apologized and explained the situation. The elk offered to help find the keys under the snowy mess. Ned told him about the penguin traps.

"Not a problem," said the elk. "I eat penguin traps for breakfast."

This comment led to a thirty minute exchange of recipes between Ned and the elk before Ned finally agreed to let the elk help find the keys.

Angora was once again standing next to Ned and once again she nudged him with her knuckles.

"Oh, that's right," said Ned. "That wouldn't be a good idea. I enjoy hunting elk too much. If I see you in my backyard – well you wouldn't be safe from my love of hunting elk."

The elk left. The snow started to fall again so the doorbell didn't ring again.

When the snowy mess melted, the keys to the planet booth were nowhere near what had been Ned and Angora's happy azalea bed.

The keys had been in the butter dish next to their three-platter toaster all the time. Ned had been on the defensive and Angora on the offensive most of the winter, so neither of them thought to look there.

THE AGREEABLE GIRAFFE

A forest of tall oak trees greeted Heinrich and his giraffe on their way through the countryside.

"These oak trees mean that we are getting closer to the village," said Heinrich.

5

"This means we are getting closer indeed," agreed the giraffe.

Suddenly, Otto the trader emerged from the oak trees to greet the two travelers.

"That is a fine-looking giraffe," said Otto.

"Yes, yes, I am a fine-looking giraffe indeed," agreed the giraffe.

"And such an agreeable giraffe also," added Otto.

"Yes, yes, I am quite agreeable," agreed the giraffe.

"I will trade you a bag of silver and my elk here for your giraffe," offered Otto.

"What elk?" asked Heinrich. "I see no elk."

"I don't see any elk either," said the giraffe.

"Hey, you stupid elk!" shouted Otto. "Get over here."

Otto's elk emerged from behind the oaks.

"As you can see, this is a fine elk," said Otto.

"Yes, yes, probably the finest in the forest," agreed the giraffe.

"But my giraffe is very agreeable," countered Heinrich. "He is incredibly rare."

"Yes, yes, you don't find many giraffes like me anywhere," agreed the giraffe.

"Is your elk an agreeable elk?" asked Heinrich.

The elk stared at Otto who was suddenly quiet.

"Should I tell this rube the truth?" asked the elk. Otto didn't answer, so the elk answered Heinrich's question, "You seem like a rather stupid fellow and you smell funny too. Otto here is trying to swindle you and get rid of me."

"Yes, yes, that seems like what Otto is trying to do here," agreed the giraffe.

Otto was crestfallen. His chance to get rid of his rude elk and gain the agreeable giraffe had apparently gone down in flames. There was an uncomfortable silence.

"It's a deal!" shouted Heinrich and he took Otto's bag of silver.

Otto was startled and said nothing as he watched Heinrich take the elk and wander through the forest until the two were out of sight.

"Okay, this is where you and I go our separate ways," Heinrich told the elk.

"This is good because you seem rather creepy to me," said the elk before disappearing into the forest.

Heinrich continued his travels and saw a village in the distance. He smiled, happy to be rid of the grumpy elk and the boring giraffe, and even happier that his new bag of silver gave him the opportunity to buy a better companion.

THE SPIDER THAT EMBRACED US

My wife and I were discussing ideas for my next short story when we heard a high-pitched voice coming from the top of the far corner of the dining room.

"I embrace the two of you," said the spider that was the source of the high-pitched voice.

"Embrace us?" asked my wife, apparently not concerned that she was having a conversation with a spider.

"I mean that I support your discussion and his writing efforts," explained the spider. "I enjoyed all three of the stories he read, even though there were no spiders in them. In fact, if I may be so bold as to suggest, you really should consider including spiders in your stories. We are an eclectic bunch, well suited to being literary characters.

"We still need to goosh you," my wife said, almost apologetically. "We have rules in this house."

"Not so fast, dear," I interjected. "I hadn't thought about having spiders in my stories. That is certainly worth considering."

"Did you notice that the spider is building a web in the far corner of our dining room?" my wife asked me.

"Sorry, it's an occupational hazard," explained the spider.

"Perhaps we could give the spider amnesty," I suggested to my wife.

"Amnesty?" she asked.

"Yes, perhaps safe passage to our neighbor's house."

"No, that won't do," said the spider. "Their house is too clean. They don't get flies like you do."

"Oh, that's it!" said my wife angrily. "There's definitely going to be a gooshing!"

In the division of labor in our house, spider gooshing is among my responsibilities, along with getting dishes off the top shelves and fluffing up the pillows on the couch before football games on TV.

"I'll get the swatter," I said as my wife went to watch TV.

"Get on the swatter," I whispered to the spider. I opened the sliding glass doors and escorted him to the wall between our house and our neighbors, the not-as-neat ones.

"Once again, I embrace you," said the spider. "You are a good person, and your wife – even with her anti-spider prejudice – knows how to make a home hospitable for spiders. Yes, I shall tell all my friends about the two of you."

After hearing those words, I decided to take his advice and write my next story about a spider. I also decided that gooshing him right then and there would be a good way to end that story.

Steve Pastis is a writer living in Visalia, California. He has written for the *Valley Voice*, *The Good Life*, *Greek Accent*, *Farm News*, *Custom Boat & Engine*, *Baseball Cards*, *Circus*, *Rock Fever*, *Occidental Magazine*, *Happening Magazine*, *Destination Visalia*, *South Valley Networking*, *Hellenic Calendar*, and *Cool and Strange Music*. His short stories have been published in *The Journal of Experimental Fiction*, *Signs of Life*, and *Gargoyle*. Two of his short story collections, *Fables for the Clarinet* and *Ten Good Reasons to Fix that Airplane*, are available on Amazon. His website, NameYourOwnDuck.com will eventually be up and running, honest.

THE MEMORY TREE

CHRISTINE L. VILLA

SNOWBALL FRIEND

snowball fur
sitting on my lap . . .
how easily
my couch welcomes
another stranger

waxing moon . . .
the winter silence
turns into
the pitter patter
of puppy paws

our gazes
locked to each other . . .
letting go
of my long list
of household rules

my carpet stained
with the trial and error
of potty training . . .
the spring rain rinses
the day's grime

I cling to the scent
of her lavender bath . . .
both shivering

I ask her if she too
will leave me one day

*This is a tanka sequence which was first published in *Ribbons* Fall/Winter 2017 Volume 13, Number 2. A tanka is a small lyrical poem that is written in thirty-one or fewer syllables in five rhythmic lines, often with a pivot line of some kind, and seeks to leave something out so that it may be implied, usually with intuitive or emotional effect. As it was over 1,200 years ago, it mostly deals with human relationships or the author's situation. It has always been a poem of feelings, often involving metaphor and other figurative language (not generally used in haiku). The best tanka poems harmonize the writer's emotional life with the elements of the outer world.

THE MEMORY TREE

*This children's story was originally intended for a picture book. It had been published in a newspaper and magazine. It was first published in *Misamis Star Express* (December 2010), a newspaper in the Philippines. The second publication is in *Lighter Chatter* (May 2012), a monthly magazine of Lamplighter Mobile Home Park in North Highlands, CA. Since pictures are not allowed to be included here, please imagine the two main characters as squirrels.

"Hi, little Susie!" greeted Mindy. "Here's a sunflower for you!"

"Gee, thank you," said Susie. "You're one special friend! I'm going to keep this in my secret treasure box. Mom said I can collect memories and keep them."

Susie showed Mindy her secret treasure box.

"Wow! What other memories are in there?" asked Mindy.

Susie smiled and answered, "A heart locket with Mom and Dad's picture, a music box from Grandma, a candy cane from my first winter, and a strawberry."

"Why are you keeping that strawberry?" asked Mindy.

"It's a reminder of how much fun I had picking some strawberries. On my way home, I dipped them in a chocolate pond."

"You sure have one treasure box filled with happy memories," said Mindy.

"Absolutely! And I'm keeping them forever!" Susie clutched the treasure box close to her heart.

Susie dug a hole under a bush and hid her treasure box. She made sure she knew which bush it was. It was the bush closest to the running brook.

Fall came and went by quickly. All the leaves changed colors and fell on the ground. Soon a thick blanket of snow covered everything.

"Do we really have to find your treasure box now? I'm freezing!" whined Mindy.

"I know it's just right here," said Susie.

"But we've been looking for an hour. Why not wait for the snow to melt? I'm-I'm sure it's still gonna be-be here." Mindy's teeth started to chatter, her extra-long tail curling up into a ball.

Susie made a big sigh and said, "Okay. Let's go home."

The two friends huddled together as they pushed their way through the snow.

That night Susie sadly watched the snowflakes fall. She was worried that her treasure box was gone. When will the snowflakes stop falling? What if she never found her treasure box? Will she forget all her happy memories?

Susie poured out all her worries to Mom.

"Just close your eyes, Susie," Mom said. "Your treasure box is right inside your heart. You'll never forget the memories."

Susie closed her eyes and felt the happiness inside her heart. Slowly, she remembered everything she had in her treasure box. In her mind, she saw her heart locket, her music box, her candy cane, her strawberry, and her sunflower. The memories that went with them were still there after all.

But what if one day that wouldn't work anymore? That would make her very, very sad. She panicked and thought that she still needed to find her treasure box.

One day, the sun was warm and the snow melted away.

Susie and Mindy searched for the bush closest to the running brook.

"The bush is gone!" exclaimed Susie.

"Look! I think it's been replaced by this strange plant. Uhmmm. It smells like strawberries?" said Mindy.

"C'mon, keep on digging. It must be right here," insisted Susie, as her little toes dug harder and harder.

They dug everywhere close to it. Still, the treasure box was nowhere to be found.

"I think I've lost it," said Susie. A teardrop plopped on a blade of grass.

"I'm sorry, little Susie. We tried our best to find it," said Mindy.

"Yeah, we did. I guess I just have to remember what Mom said."

From then on, Susie did just that. Whenever she started missing her old treasure box, she just closed her eyes and felt the happiness inside. Sometimes it worked. Sometimes it didn't. Until one sunny afternoon, after a year went by, the strange plant magically grew taller and bigger.

"Look, Mindy! It's my memory tree!" Susie ran up the tree and Mindy chased after her. They marveled at how beautiful the tree was. It blossomed with sunflowers, candy canes, and chocolate-covered strawberries. The tree was even softly playing a merry melody. And when a slight breeze blew by, a puff of strawberry scent filled the air.

"This is awesome, Susie! It sure is your memory tree," said Mindy, "but what if... what if the tree dies one day?"

Susie saw the heart etched on the center of the trunk. It was her heart locket. It reminded her to smile and to believe. The heart truly never forgets. Now all her worries went away. And this time it was for good.

"I'm not worried about it," said Susie. She picked up a sunflower and gave it to Mindy. "Whatever happens, my memories will stay with me forever." She closed her eyes and felt warm inside.

Mindy's extra-long tail curled upwards. She understood

what Susie meant. They circled the trunk and started chasing each other on the branches of the tree and around the candy canes, the chocolate-covered strawberries, and the sunflowers.

Christine "Chrissi" L. Villa is the founder of *Purple Cotton Candy Arts*, a small business that started out to explore her creativity in the field of arts and crafts and later expanded into publishing her children's picture books. She has published nine children's book titles since 2014, two of which won first place in the Northern California Publishers and Authors Book Award Competition in 2018 and 2019. Recently, *Purple Cotton Candy Arts* started offering publishing services to other aspiring children's authors and publishers.

As a gifted poet, Chrissi's haiku and tanka have appeared in numerous online and print journals worldwide. She has garnered several awards and has published her first poetry book entitled *The Bluebird's Cry*. She is the founding editor of *Frameless Sky*— the very first haiku and tanka video journal available in DVD. She has launched a haiku book by another author under her own imprint, *Velvet Dusk Publishing*.

JOCKO, A CAT FOR ALL SEASONS

BOB IRELAN

A number of best-selling books tell heartwarming, often humorous stories about the life and times of a dog or cat and the lives they touched. Those I've read are sensitively and well written and deliver memorable messages about loyalty, courage, and love. But, sadly, most seem to be penned after the principal character has died.

I don't want to wait until my cat, Jocko, meets his maker. First, he may well outlast me; I'm 82 and Jocko's 16 (I don't know what that converts to in "cat years," but let's say we're contemporaries). And, second, if I don't write at least my modest part of his story, who will?

Jocko entered into my life in a rather unconventional way. I had cats as a boy living in the Maryland countryside. My favorite was Figaro, a carousing, never-neutered, grey and white tomcat who lived to be 15 or 16. However, after my beloved Barbara and I married in 1959, cats were not a part of our life. My mother-in-law was afraid of them, saying she had been clawed as a child. Knowing that history, my introducing a feline into the family probably would have sent a negative message. So, no cats. That changed in November of 2007, when – without warning – Barbara said a friend was dying and was very anxious to find a happy home for her cat. "Do you want to take a look at him?"

"Sure," I answered, sharing her sadness that a friend was terminally ill but surprised my beloved might be interested in adding to our family. Thinking back now, I shouldn't have been surprised because Barbara was always someone whose heart was unselfish and whose friendship could be counted on.

A short time later, we visited Jocko. Barbara held him in

her arms, he purred, and the decision to adopt was immediate. Was it fate or coincidence that he bore the same not-so-common name as my childhood stuffed toy monkey? You decide.

At this point I should describe Jocko. He's an American shorthair. I believe he qualifies as a Tuxedo or Jellico because he is black with a white chest and white feet. Whatever...he's a handsome boy and seems to know it. And, he's living proof of the behavioral description that, while dogs have owners, cats have staff.

The chemistry between Jocko and me developed quickly, which was a bit of a surprise since his previous staff was a woman. He was a little more "reserved" with Barbara for a while, teasing her by running away most of the times when she tried to pick him up. She never quite got used to Jocko not always responding to her "come" urgings. But they bonded, on his terms of course.

Jocko quickly became an investment/cost center as well as a welcomed physical presence. A week after his no-cost adoption, we took him to the vet for his annual booster shots. During the course of an examination, the vet determined Jocko had a badly abscessed tooth.

"It's got to come out," the vet said. "And the rest need a good cleaning." A couple of days later – post dental surgery and cleaning – we owned a $990.33 kitty. Thank God he didn't need orthodontics.

Ten months later, a shock and sadness the likes of which I'd never experienced came crashing down. Without warning and after nearly 50 years of marriage, Barbara collapsed and died of a massive heart attack while playing golf. Life would change forever. The years of wonderful memories and the floodtide of love and support of children, grandchildren, and friends were incredible strengths, but the feeling of loss and emptiness was heavy. I tried to concentrate on how blessed I was to have been her spouse and best friend for so long, but even that couldn't totally displace the selfish sadness I felt.

That's when "the Jocko effect" took hold to a degree I

could never have foreseen. He was my companion, my pal. He was, after all, with me because of my beloved life partner. He was yet another gift from her. His company, his curling up with me, his nudging and walking all over me to get me up and going in the morning were medicines the efficacy of which no doctor could prescribe.

Earlier, I had begun carrying him outside several times a day. He is, by edict, an indoor cat, but he possesses an outdoor state of mind. I'm sure he'd like nothing better than to deliver a freshly caught mouse or bird to me. But he knows nothing about the dangers of traffic or threatening critters, so our forays are always with him in my arms – even to the extent of my holding him up to his favorite tree so he can sharpen his claws. Passing neighbors are kind enough not to comment on this bizarre scene.

I've thought a lot about the Jocko connection and I've drawn some conclusions. I now believe Barbara somehow knew she would be taken from me and knew how lost I would be living alone. Why else would she suggest, after all those years of never having a cat, we adopt one? Yes, I believe she knew. And this belief only adds to the love I feel for her.

For Jocko and me, life marches on. When I sit, he most often settles in my lap. When I first go to bed, he jumps on my chest, fidgets until he's comfortable, then kneads me until I holler out in pain or he tires of it. After that, he's off to a sofa (most of the time, he's the only one who uses the formal living room) or to a windowsill or another bed. When he figures I've slept enough (think 4:30 or 5 a.m.), he returns, jumps back onto the bed, meows, climbs over me, and proceeds with however many head butts it takes to prompt my petting him. I've tried faking continued sleep; it doesn't work.

A year or so ago he decided his persuasive powers were strengthened if he became more vocal. Since then, his meows are both loud and rapid-fire.

Jocko's energy level exceeds mine – when he's awake. Nearing 17, he draws special joy from racing up and down the hall, stopping to sharpen his claws on the carpet and look over his shoulder as I clap my hands and, without effect, command, "No."

Every day Jocko makes me laugh and reminds me of the warmth and simplicity of companionship. He can't know "the story behind the story" of why he means so much to me. But, for sure, I can and I do.

 Bob Irelan's commitment to writing began in earnest when, as a student, he majored in journalism at the University of Maryland, and it grew steadily throughout his career. Following 10 years of newspaper and magazine reporting and editing, including stints at The Wall Street Journal and Nation's Business magazine in Washington, DC, he spent 32 years in public relations for a Fortune 500 family of companies. As a corporate officer, he directed the companies' internal and external communications for the last 12 of those years.

In retirement, he taught a public relations course for two years at University of the Pacific and for five years at University of California, Davis, Extension.

He is the author of a novel, *Angel's Truth – One Teenager's Quest for Justice*, published in 2018. *Angel's Truth* took second place in Fiction at NCPA's 25th Book Awards in 2019.

Bob lives with his cat, Jocko, in Rancho Murieta, California.

JUNGLE EXPEDITION

AMY ROGERS

I knew I wasn't in Sacramento any more when the tarantula marched across the dining table.

Don't kid yourself—this wasn't because we don't have tarantulas in Northern California. We do. Never seen one? Head to the Sierra foothills in October and take a look around after dusk, when spider love is in the air. Male tarantulas by the hundreds emerge from their lairs in search of eight-legged beauties.

But I digress. With this tarantula, I knew I was far from home and among a different sort of people when my fellow diners squealed with delight. A scrum formed as we all tried to get closer to the uninvited guest. If that spider had dropped in hoping to cause a good scare, it failed miserably. As we oooh'd and aaah'd and snapped photos, one woman managed to scoop up the furry arachnid on a plate barely larger than it was. She gently deposited it in the jungle that surrounded our open-air dining room, and I returned with my husband Jay to a platter of chicken and plantains.

This was our first night at the eco-lodge in Tambopata, a national ecologic reserve of the western Amazon in the country of Peru. Like the other travelers in our group, we were nature enthusiasts who'd spent the hours of a boat ride that day scanning the water and air for life. Later in the trip we might yawn at yet another wild iguana catching some sun on a high branch, but today every plant and animal was exotic and exciting. I had focused my attention on the shoreline in search of caimans, an alligator-like lizard common in that region, while opening my peripheral vision to a possible flash of color from a flock of macaws. The arrival of a tarantula at dinner was part of the fun.

After a brief introductory lecture about pumas and tapirs and toucans and every grade-school boy's favorite, titi monkeys, Jay and I retired to our private quarters in a clearing nearby. The hut had straw-covered walls and a sheet metal roof over two twin beds draped in mosquito nets. Its windows were raw openings with rough-hewn wood shutters that barely separated inside from out. I also noticed a sizable gap between the top of the door and the roof.

Well, I thought, it's more secure than a tent.

I climbed into bed, a constant thin film of sweat covering me in the humid air. The darkness was thick. Unfamiliar noises surrounded me, sounds not only strange, but *loud*. Even if my brain hadn't been flitting hither and thither trying to make sense of them all, the sheer volume would've been enough to keep me awake. Jungle at dusk is a noisy place. Mosquitoes buzzed with frustration on the other side of my protective net. Tropical frogs chirped and sang. Far-off howler monkeys roared. By some miracle, Jay snored.

As time passed, the jungle quieted. I squinted for the hand I could not see in front of my face, smelled the fecund air, and listened. There was a soft sound I had missed earlier, or maybe it had just begun? A whisper of frictionless movement. I concentrated my functioning senses. Left. Right. Left. The tiniest breeze.

"Jay?" I whispered. Then I said it again, a bit louder.

He stirred. "Huh?"

"I think there's a bat in here."

We both listened to whatever it was swooping back and forth above us.

"Cool," he said.

I covered my head with a sheet. "Right."

Jay was soon back to snoring.

Well, I thought, they do eat mosquitoes.

Whoosh. Whoosh. Tiny squeak.

If they were vampire bats, I reasoned, they wouldn't be flying to catch their prey. But I bundled the sheet around my neck.

Eventually the bats moved on to whatever else bats do in the jungle at night. Jay's sleep deepened into silence. The moon must have come up outside as the barest hint of light entered the hut. This was not an improvement, as now my imagination "saw" movements in the murky shades of dark.

At some point I must have dozed off because a noise startled me awake. A rustling and crackling, of foliage being parted and crushed.

My heart pounded. Something was at the window.

I grabbed the edges of my bed. What sort of creature could it be? I heard it move along the edge of the hut toward the door. Whatever it was, it was *big*. Excited, my mind conjured wild suggestions. An elephant? Duh. No. A bear? I couldn't remember if there was some kind of tropical bear in this region.

The animal made a chuffing sound, its breath loud and close. A jaguar?

There were jaguars in the park, for sure. And they were active at night. Could it be? I desperately wanted to see a big cat. Should I get up and look? Could I find my way in the dark? Half of me was afraid I would scare the animal away. Half of me was afraid I would not.

Well, I thought, getting eaten by a jaguar would be a hell of a way to go.

Undecided, I lay still and listened. The creature moved off a bit, and I heard the sound of ripping and tearing leaves. Not a jaguar, then. Capybara, a hundred-pound jungle rodent? Or even a giant anteater rooting around?

Out of either fear or wisdom, I didn't leave my bed until dawn. Then I grabbed Jay to help me search the area around the hut for clues, as if I were some kind of big-game tracker. Sure. There was grass. There were oversized leafy plants around the huts. And there was pockmarked mud. Of course we didn't learn a thing.

Eager to make an ID of the nighttime visitor so I could check it off my bucket list of Rainforest Animal Encounters on this trip, I skipped over to breakfast. I proudly told my story to another American woman on the trip. She was immediately struck by a tropical bout of FOMO—fear of missing out—and vowed to stay awake late tonight. As we grazed through a lovely buffet of ripe papayas and local bananas, I spotted our group leader, a naturalist with decades of experience in the area, and repeated my tale.

"That was Esmeralda," she said with confidence.

My pulse quickened. They've named it—it's a regular visitor! "Will Esmeralda be back again tonight? Is she tame enough to let me get a photo?"

She laughed. "Yes, she is. She belongs to the lodge owner."

Oh, these jungle people and their exotic pets! "Is Esmeralda an agouti? A peccary?"

"A horse."

"A pygmy horse?" I hadn't heard such a creature mentioned in any of the eco-literature, so it must be very rare indeed.

"A *horse* horse," Jay said, appearing at the buffet. "I just saw it grazing around the huts."

I never did spot a jaguar on that trip but I have some killer close-ups of a sorrel mare, if you'd like to see them sometime.

Amy Rogers, MD, PhD, is a Harvard-educated scientist, novelist, journalist, educator, critic, and publisher who specializes in all things science-y. Her thriller novels *Petroplague, Reversion,* and *The Han Agent* use real science and medicine to create plausible, frightening scenarios. Formerly a microbiology professor at CSU-Sacramento, she is an active member of International Thriller Writers, and serves as treasurer for Northern California Publishers and Authors. In addition, she runs the ScienceThrillers.com genre book review website. Amy lives in Sacramento with a herd of house cats and loves to get outside. Learn more at AmyRogers.com.

MOUSE DROPPINGS

ELAINE FABER

They looked like raisins, but she knew they were mouse droppings. On the porch–on the bookshelf–on the floor. *My Santa Barbara home doesn't have mice!* But it wasn't her home anymore since the divorce. The final blow? While she was hospitalized, Doug gave away her brown and white terrier, Waffles.

He'd said, "I can't take care of a dog. It'll be hard enough taking care of you." Then, he filed for divorce and the house had to be sold. Paying off the credit cards took half of the proceeds.

She blinked back tears. Couldn't Doug see she was getting better? Why did he leave when she needed him most? Hadn't he promised *in sickness and in health*?

She glanced around the Tahoe cabin her cousin, Michael, had loaned her for the summer. All the comforts of home: hand-made log furniture, a 30" color TV, and a leather sofa. She could imagine a crackling fire in the pot-belly stove on a cold, snowy night and...wait! Was that more mouse droppings on the top of the pot-belly? *Yuck!*

The kitchen window over-looked a redwood deck and a babbling creek. Birds chirped in the towering pines. *Just beautiful!* She slid open the kitchen window. The scent of fresh pines dulled the ache in her heart. Perhaps spending the next few months in this lovely haven would be just what she needed. Gina carried her mug of tea onto the redwood deck, collapsed in a lawn chair, and closed her eyes.

Silence...except for the occasional bird twitter and the trickling stream. Occasionally, a car rumbled past the cabin. Even the cabin next door was shuttered and quiet. Tomorrow, she'd go into town and deal with the physical therapist her doctor recommended. *Tonight, I'll simply enjoy the peace and quiet.* When the sun went down, the cabin quickly chilled in the mountain shade. Gina put in a DVD and settled onto the sofa with a comforter.

Scratch – scratch.

Gina jolted upright. *What was that?* Just outside the door! Was someone breaking in?

The TV screen flickered snow. She swallowed down the throbbing in her ears and listened. *I must have fallen asleep.*

Scratch, scratch.

"It's that darn mouse. And, now I have a crick in my neck." Gina gripped the railing with her right hand as she climbed the stairs, one step at a time. Left foot. Right foot, left. She couldn't have climbed the stairs when she was released from the hospital just three weeks ago following a stroke. She *was* improving. She crawled into bed, convinced she wouldn't sleep a wink.

Sun streamed through the window and crept across her face. She stretched and yawned.

"You shouldn't blame yourself, you know," said a small voice, somewhere across the room.

Gina sat upright. "What? Who said that?"

"It's just me."

Her gaze circled the room and stopped at the dresser where a little brown mouse sat, his whiskers atwitch. She pulled the covers up around her neck. "What–?"

"I said it's not your fault."

"What do you mean, not my...what am I saying? You're a mouse. How can you...?" Her lips trembled. "Am I dreaming?" Her cold fingers touched her cheek.

"Don't worry, you're awake. *Ahem!* I *said* you aren't to blame for the divorce."

Gina's ears buzzed and the walls looked a little swishy. *I must be dreaming...talking to a mouse.* Okay. She was stressed. "How could a mouse be talking?"

"It's not unheard of." He raised a tiny foot and ticked off

23

one toe after another. "Let's see now. You've got Mickey Mouse, Mighty Mouse and Tom and Jerry. No, wait! I think Tom was a cat. That leaves Jerry. They all talked."

Gina pinched her arm. *Ouch.* Awake, but obviously hallucinating. "Mickey Mouse and Mighty Mouse are cartoon characters." Her short curls bobbed as she shook her head. "Pretty sure real mice don't talk."

"You were pretty sure Doug would stick by you, but look how that turned out."

Gina nodded. The mouse was right. "You've got me there. But, you're wrong. It's all my fault." Tears pricked her eyes. "If I didn't get sick, my husband wouldn't have divorced me and given away Waffles." It hurt even more to say it out loud.

The mouse again ticked off each item as he spoke. "By that logic, if you didn't work at Crusens, you wouldn't have met Doug, so when you got sick, he could divorce you and give away your dog. So, it must be Crusens' fault for hiring you in the first place. Did you file for Worker's Compensation?"

"Don't be silly. That's ridiculous." Gina reached for a glass of water on the nightstand.

"You think you're so clever, don't you?" When she turned back toward the wee creature had disappeared. "Where...?" Gina arose and peered under the bed. Her cheeks warmed. "I couldn't have seen..." Then she spotted...mouse droppings on the dresser. "Okay, there *was* a mouse! I saw it as I was waking up. I dreamed the rest."

* * *

After breakfast, Gina drove down the mountain road into Tahoe and located the physical therapy facility where she met with her therapist.

"I'm Jake. Come on in and let's get started, Gina. We'll meet here in the clinic three days a week and you'll have home exercises. How does that sound?"

Gina's heart did a flip-flop. Jake was so handsome. *Shame on you, Gina. Barely divorced!*

For the next hour, Jake prodded and pummeled Gina's body. Following their session, they sat on the patio and chatted over coffee.

"How long will we be working together, Gina?" Jake's blue eyes twinkled.

Was he flirting with her? "I'm returning to my job in Santa Barbara this October if I can recover enough this summer."

"That's a coincidence. I'm starting a job at the Santa Barbara Memorial Hospital this fall."

Gina nodded. "I should have said I hope to return to my job." Her coffee sloshed when she slammed her cup onto the table. "Who has a stroke at the age of thirty-seven?"

"Take it easy, Gina! It's not your fault you had a stroke!"

Gina's head jerked up. "That's odd. That's the second time I've heard that today." She shook her head. "My friend, Marian, used to say, *Cheer up. Things will get better.*"

"Sounds like she cared about you. That was good advice."

"Easy to say when you aren't homeless, crippled and abandoned." She blinked back the tears threatening to spill down her cheeks. "Then Marian kisses me good-bye, and walks her perfect size eight body back to her perfect husband, while I return to..." She shrugged. "I know. I'm just feeling sorry for myself and getting all emotional again."

Jake touched her arm. "We've got all summer. I'm good at my job. I promise we'll get your strength back." He stood and checked his watch. "I've got another appointment. We'll talk again Friday. Take it easy driving home."

Gina's lip trembled. "Thanks, Jake. I'll see you Friday."

Jake's words were encouraging, but driving up the hill, her thoughts filled with doubts again. Would Crusens hold her job until her strength improved enough to return to work?

Once inside the quiet cabin, she flung herself onto the sofa. *I won't give in. I won't! I miss Waffles so much. I'm so alone and I—*

"Why don't you call her?"

"*Huh?*" Gina lifted her head. That voice again!

"I said you should call her." The mouse stared at her from the kitchen table. "You've thought about it. Do it."

That darn mouse, of course. "You mean Mrs. Johnson? Call about Waffles?"

"Bingo! Give the lady a cigar!"

"What good would it do? He's probably forgotten me by now."

"As sure as pigs fly…"

"She wouldn't let me have him back now, would she?" Gina sat up straighter.

"Who knows? Why don't you ask? What have you got to lose?"

"Okay, I'll do it. *Hey!* Get off the kitchen table, for Pete's sake!"

The mouse wiggled his whiskers and scurried onto the floor.

Gina grabbed the phone, called *Information*, and dialed the phone number. "Hi, Mrs. Johnson? This is Gina. How are things?"

"Gina! We're fine. We were just thinking about you this morning. How are you getting along?"

"I'm okay. I'm spending the summer at my cousin's cabin in Tahoe. *Umm…*" Gina's heart pounded. "How's Waffles?"

"He's great, but isn't it a coincidence you called? You see, Jeff has a job offer in the Bay Area, but rent is so high, all we can afford is a condo. I'm afraid we can't keep Waffles. We've been meaning to call Doug. We love the little mutt, but…"

"You're kidding. I called to see if you'd give Waffles back to me!"

"Well, won't that work out fine? We'll be here for another month, so there's no hurry."

"How about next weekend? I could drive down and pick him up. Say, Saturday afternoon?"

"Fine. Whenever it's convenient. So glad this worked out. I'll see you next weekend. Good-bye, dear."

"Bye." Gina hung up the phone and turned. "How did you know? Mrs. Johnson said…"

The mouse was gone.

Gina's head whirled as she undressed for bed that night. Filled with enthusiasm toward the future, she thought of taking long walks with Waffles. Next fall, when she returned to Santa

Barbara, she'd rent an apartment where they allowed dogs. Maybe she and Jake might get together…for coffee…

She pushed back the bathroom curtain to look at the stars. A light flickered in the abandoned cabin next door, and then flicked out. The front door opened and a dark figure emerged, carrying a large bundle. The car sagged when he dropped the heavy object into the trunk.

Gina sucked in her breath. It was too dark to read the license number. The car started up the driveway and turned onto the highway. She climbed into bed, her head buzzing, puzzling out what she had just seen. *Stop it! You've been watching too many TV murder mysteries.*

It was probably a heavy rug he was taking to the cleaners. Yeah, right. At 11:30 at night? Or, maybe he was bringing firewood to the Placerville Farmer's Market. That explains it. Oh…oh, I know. It was a bundle of old clothes for the Salvation Army-uh huh. Let's face it. You know what he was doing.

The guy's wife had a stroke and he doesn't want to take care of her. He didn't even bother with a divorce. He just killed her and threw her in the trunk.

"He'll probably bury her in the woods and they'll never find her body. Most likely, he strangled her little dog, too!" Her voice echoed in the darkness.

She licked her dry lips. Should she call the police? She picked up her cell phone. *What kind of car was it? Ford? Tan? White?* She couldn't remember. Who would believe her? She couldn't identify the vehicle or the driver. All she saw was a man loading something heavy into the trunk at 11:30 P.M. But, wasn't it obvious? She pulled the covers up to her chin and whispered, "I just know he's murdered his wife and now he'll dispose of her body!" Gina picked at the bed sheet and stared out the window into the dark trees.

"Gina, that was George's son, Randy."

Somehow, hearing the mouse's voice was no surprise. Gina threw back the sheet and scooted up against the headboard. There he was, sitting on the dresser. "How do you know? What was he carrying? How can you be sure?"

"Let me see. How do I know? Because, I was over there earlier this evening. I overheard him on the phone. Randy drove in from Boise, Idaho, on his way to the San Francisco airport. He stopped at his dad's cabin to sleep for a few hours. He left at 11:30 P.M. because he leaves for Iraq early tomorrow morning. That was his duffle bag he put in the trunk. Any more questions?"

"*Uh*, no, I guess not."

"Gina, let's think about this for a minute. You have a beautiful place to live this summer while you rest and recuperate, and your boss is holding your job until you're well. You've made a new friend and you're getting Waffles back. Why are you imagining killers next door? Honey, you've got to get a grip. Stop dwelling on the negative. Concentrate on the present and look to the future."

He's right. Maybe if I stopped obsessing on myself, I wouldn't be talking to a mouse.

"You're right. I'll do better. I'll stop thinking about..." The mouse scampered away.

Gina smiled. Just two days ago, she came to the cabin, abandoned, unloved and broken in spirit. Somehow, in two short days, nothing had changed, yet everything had changed. Maybe, only her perspective had changed. The difficulties of the stroke, the divorce, losing the house and Waffles no longer felt insurmountable. They were just minor annoyances, like mouse droppings.

She had so much to look forward to. The mouse was right. She was getting stronger every day. Waffles was coming home. Her job was secure. Everything was going to be all right. Gina smiled and snuggled deeper under the covers. That's when she heard it.

SNAP!!!!

Was that a...a...mousetrap? She clapped her hands over her ears and leaped out of bed.

Oh no! "Mouse! Mouse! Where are you?"

Silence.

Gina pulled the dresser away from the wall, turned over

the wastebasket, shoved shoes around in the closet. There! The moonlight framed the small brown body mashed beneath the cruel wire. Beady eyes, lifeless and dull, stared up at her. Tears streamed down Gina's cheeks.

"Oh! Mouse!" She stroked the still warm fur with fingertips wet with tears.

His words had encouraged her…or had he ever spoken at all? Perhaps seeing the mouse had only influenced her own mind and set loose the strength and courage buried deep within her.

Either way, he had changed her outlook. Somehow, she now felt able to face her challenges and move forward. She wished she could thank him.

She thought back over all the encouragement she had received since coming to the cabin; Jake's promise to help her regain her strength. Mrs. Johnson's unexpected offer to return Waffles. Whether real or imaginary, her conversations with the mouse and his inspiring messages had helped her see a brighter future. Each had helped her move from despair toward a path of emotional healing, but none of these assurances brought her as much relief and joy as the voice she heard from across the room atop the dresser.

"Gina, I warned that young fool about the mousetrap in the closet, but what can you do with this younger generation? Have you noticed? Those darn whippersnappers? They just never listen…"

Elaine Faber lives in Northern California with her husband and feline companions. She is a member of Sisters in Crime, California Cat Writers, and Northern California Publishers and Authors. She volunteers with the American Cancer Society. She has published seven books and is included in multiple anthologies: http://www.mindcandymysteries.com.

29

OH, THAT STRAWBERRY ROAN

JUDITH VAUGHAN

I was already horse crazy.

In the spring of 1950, just after I turned six, my father drove me to a homestead that was east of Las Vegas, New Mexico, where he had recently moved our family from New Orleans to what they considered the wild west. It was a big change from suburban city life. Mother and my sisters were cautious but curious. Daddy sweetened the deal with the assurance that this life would include more horses. I was promised a horse of my own.

Today, I would try out a horse named *Babe*.

I'd ridden before—astride Daddy's horse, Lady, through the pinewoods of the South, near our weekend cottage in Mississippi. He'd ride behind me, both of us snug in the same English saddle. He'd give me the reins, and guide my hands to steer and stop.

That day, I jumped from the car and held Daddy's hand as we crossed a yard of weeds and rusting farm equipment, to a man with a grey beard who was holding a small horse in front of a tumble-down barn with fading red paint.

"A pink pony!" I said. I studied this creature that was unlike any horse I'd ever seen. Nothing on the ramshackle farm was as fine.

"Yes," Daddy said. "This is Babe. She's a strawberry roan, a very rare color. If you can ride her, Sandy, I'll buy her for you."

Babe glowed in the afternoon light. Daddy placed my hand on the horse as an introduction for both of us. She was warm and smelled of molasses. I stroked her shining purplish-pink shoulder. The little mare was just my size. I'd be able to saddle her myself. I traced the outline of the white blaze on her face. Her eyes were brown and calm. I curled my fingers into a mane as wavy as my hair. She lowered her head and rubbed it up and down my ribs. I held her neck to catch my balance. I laughed. She liked me. The old man led Babe to a mucky pen. Daddy and I followed.

No bridle…no saddle…by myself? *If I could ride her*, Daddy had said. *Then she'd be mine.* What if I couldn't?

Just a year before our move, I had begged to ride by myself. Daddy resisted, but finally began some short lessons on his tall Tennessee walking horse. I sat up and beamed as Lady walked on.

Daddy brought Mother out to watch me, but when Lady sped up, I fell off into the mud and cried. Mother scooped me up and carried me to the cottage, her face worried. After that, only my sister would lift me on to her old horse Smokey to plod along and practice riding solo.

Ready or not, Daddy gave me a boost by my left knee. As he lifted me higher, I grabbed Babe's red mane and swung myself onto her bare back. I took the halter rope as a rein. I met my father's gaze.

If Babe with her magical coat were to become my own horse in our new home in cowboy country, I had to pass this test.

"You'll be fine," my father said.

Babe shook her head and stepped off along the fence line of the pen. In my stiff new jeans and my unscuffed western boots, my hands felt unsure and my head light. I guided her through a figure eight. That wasn't so bad. The mare's unhurried trot did not shake me. Now my body moved with Babe. My hands steadied. I clicked with my tongue and kicked her sides. She moved to a lope, and together we wheeled around the pen like birds on the wind. The shabby farm faded away.

I settled into Babe's delicious rhythm. I found Daddy's face

31

as he stood next to the pen. He mirrored my confidence with a sparkle in his eyes.

"That's Babe's rocking chair lope," the grizzled man said.

I dismounted, smiling and taking short breaths that bubbled over into chuckles.

Daddy shook hands with me. "A blue-ribbon ride," he said, pulled me into a hug and gave the man fifty dollars. Babe was mine.

Oh, That Strawberry Roan. I knew the cowboy song, always on the radio. I had my cow pony, and I'd be a cowgirl. I couldn't fall asleep that night or the next waiting to ride her again, to stroke her silky coat, and slip her a handful of oats.

When we returned to the dilapidated farm, Daddy helped me saddle Babe, and then tacked up Lady for our first ride on the gravel roads near the old barn.

Lady walked much faster than Babe. My pony-sized mare fell behind. Daddy reined Lady in to wait for us. I kicked and clucked to Babe, and she trotted back to Lady. But then she lagged again. And again.

"I'll have to lead you if you if don't make Babe keep up," Daddy said. "You have to be the boss of your horse."

I was tired of kicking her. She was tired, too. Lady was bigger and faster. What could be done about that?

I stretched my heels down her sides and gave the strongest squeeze I could. Babe moved into a gallop. We flew back to Daddy, and Babe managed to stay beside Lady's fast running walk at a canter, the rocking horse lope. Daddy beamed.

On the next ride, we rode farther and faster. I loved the constant lope—I was flying.

One day, when I clucked my tongue for more speed, my short-legged mare stopped. I kicked and shook the reins. She stood, her legs stiff, and ignored me. Then Babe put her ears back, whirled on her hind legs, and leapt away from Daddy and Lady, sprinting in a gallop as fast as she could go.

I pulled back on the reins. "Whoa!" I shouted. "Babe, whoa!" All my fifty-pound strength could not stop or turn her. "Whoa!" She ran all the way back to the farm, ducked into the gate of the homestead and stopped just short of the barn. Daddy followed us in, Lady rearing and snorting after the chase. Breathless and shaky, I looked at Daddy with a crazy grin. What a wild ride. I should have been scared. I hadn't fallen off. But why would she run off like that? Daddy frowned. He wiped sweat off his forehead. My grin faded. I hadn't been the boss of my little mare. Could I ever be? The strawberry roan in the song was an outlaw bronc. Would Daddy take Babe away from me? Not let me keep her to move with us to our new horse farm in the mountains?

My dad dismounted from Lady, lifted me off Babe, and hugged me to his chest. Our breath rose and fell as our racing heartbeats slowed together. Babe lowered her head and grazed on the weeds. She was no outlaw.

Daddy didn't scold me, but the next ride, he snapped a lead rope onto Babe's bridle. After a mile or two, I pleaded, "Take the rope off, Daddy. I feel like a baby. Babe'll be good."

We hadn't gone another mile before Babe bolted again. "Whoa, Babe," I cried with all my authority as she galloped home. I did everything Daddy told me to stop her—kept my heels away from her sides, sat up straight, and reined back with all my strength. Scared? I was too busy. I had to solve this.

Again, and again, Babe ran home whenever she tired of the latest ride. I jerked the reins; I pounded my fists into her neck. Nothing deterred her. But I stayed on, and I didn't cry. "You old cuss," I said.

Daddy became quiet about me and Babe. Was he mad at me? At Babe? I knew he was worried, and if I couldn't control her soon…I couldn't bear to lose Babe. I would face any challenge for this spirited, elegant, strawberry roan mare.

"You need an equalizer," said Daddy as we got ready for the next ride. He showed me a new bridle for Babe. "I saw this advertised in the *Western Horseman*," he said. "It came in the mail today."

I loved the magazine for western riders, and watched as he

fitted the patented E-Z Stop Hackamore onto Babe's head. Instead of a bit in the horse's mouth, the hackamore had a leather-covered noseband backed by a lever attached to the reins.

"It's like Babe can't—or won't—hear what you're saying, Sandy," Daddy said. "The hackamore raises the volume of your message to stop."

Soon after we began our next ride, Babe slowed and lagged. The bolt was coming…she stopped and whirled, shifting her weight to her hind legs, ready for the leap into the gallop home. I was ready, too. I sat up straight, and shortened the reins.

As I steadied the reins, the mare raised her head and sensed the pressure of the hackamore. She shook her nose, and flexed her neck. I felt not the wrenching bolt, but a few mincing steps, like a circus horse dancing to music. Babe stopped. I eased the pressure. The mare relaxed. I urged her forward, and she let me guide her away from the direction of the barn. She could hear me! I stopped her again. She was listening! I looked over to Daddy, and chuckled as Babe two-stepped again.

No shouts of whoa, no cussing her out. Daddy was beaming. On we went. Lady in her speed walk, Babe alongside in the rocking-horse lope.

She never bolted again. She would carry me down the narrowest trail, or jump an old rock wall. Did my little mare know she was licked? That I was boss? It didn't seem so. We rode the mesas as one. Sleek and fit, Babe was having as much fun as I was.

But when I galloped up and down the steep-sided ravines—cowgirl roller coasters to me—Daddy took Babe's side.

"Would *you* like to run up and down those hills?"

"Use light hands."

"Don't cowboy her so much."

"Always walk the last mile home."

In time, I learned that I was the steward of my horse more than the master. Babe and I had become partners. After a few years of using the hackamore, I'd ride her without a bridle.

After I saw trick riders at the rodeo, I tried for weeks to ride standing up. When I fell off over Babe's shoulder again and again, she stopped and waited for me to get back on. I was the crazy one, and she was the rock.

As we both grew into our teens, I rode her less, spending hours training the colts born on our horse ranch. Babe joined the brood mare band, and produced three colts. Sired by a Tennessee Walking Horse, they grew into fast-moving trail horses that never suffered Babe's frustration of lagging behind. They had her blaze face and friendly disposition, but none were her distinctive roan color.

In 1962, during my first year of college, I received a message to call my father. Hm. Probably not good news. The note shaking in my hands, I called collect from the phone in the hall of my dorm.

"It's Babe," Daddy said. "She's developed an infection on her leg." My eyes filled with tears. I knew what was coming. "It's not responded to treatment. And now she's not comfortable standing."

"Will we have to put her down?"

"That's why I called. The vet recommends it. I wanted you to have a say."

"I don't want her to be in pain."

"I'm so sorry, honey."

I slid to the floor and began to sob. My roommate brought a box of tissues and I blubbered out the story.

"Your first horse?" she asked. "The pink one that made you a horsewoman?"

"Yes, that one. Babe, my beautiful strawberry roan."

Judy Vaughan grew up in Northern New Mexico engrossed in her father's horse breeding hobby. She left the family ranch for boarding school in Colorado and then attended Carleton College and the University of New Mexico School of Medicine. She has composed stories, mostly on horseback, since childhood, and began to hone the craft of writing ten years ago after forty years practicing medicine. She lives in Elk Grove, California, and writes with Elk Grove Writers and Artists. Works in progress include her New Mexico memoir, *Strawberry Roan* and two novels. Her story, *The Last Watermelon in Mora* placed third in the 2018 Sacramento Writers (CWC) Short Story Contest. She has three children and six grandchildren. Contact her at jfbvaughan@comcast.net.

LIZARD LOVE

SHARON S DARROW

My daughter is an addict. It hurts to admit that, but it's true. There's no cure for her addiction, no twelve-step program, and no medication that can wean her off her habit. That's right, this beautiful, intelligent woman has succumbed to the siren song of LLS, Lizard Love Syndrome. Many specialists insist that LLS is nothing but a gateway to the dreaded RCD, Reptile Collectors Disease. Never heard of RCD? Just imagine a house filled with reptiles of every imaginable type, together with live insects and rodents for food. Then imagine life with every minute and every dime devoted to nothing but the reptiles. In its final stages, the RCD sufferer can often be found haunting street corners begging for greens, worms, or crickets. We, her twin teenage sons and I, watch her like a hawk for signs that she's headed in that direction.

Like most addiction stories, my daughter – we'll call her Thelma to avoid the humiliation and judgment that plagues addicts who are outed in public – started out with one harmless little step. Her boys talked her into taking a trip to the pet store to buy pet lizards with money they'd saved. After studying every single animal, they each selected two leopard geckos since they couldn't choose between all the pretty patterns. The little animals were friendly and soon settled into their new homes. Thelma was as fascinated as her sons. In fact, she made a pest of herself by always wanting to hold and play with the new arrivals. When the boys insisted that the geckos were their pets, not hers, she headed back to the pet store in a huff, insisting she'd get her own if they wouldn't share. Who would have dreamed this was the start of it all?

Within two weeks, there were eight geckos in the house.

By the time another month passed, Thelma had researched everything she could find online about leopard geckos and joined multiple gecko owner support groups on Facebook. If only she had stopped there, Thelma might have remained a simple lizard social dabbler. Instead, she noticed that a couple of the geckos were getting fat. By this time she'd become a regular at a local reptile store where she purchased gecko food and supplies. I understand that people suffering from LLS and even RCD are not breaking the law, but I think these places should be more responsible when they see someone sliding into addiction!

Thelma took all the geckos in for examination by one of the experts, learned that every single one was female, and four were pregnant! Virgin births? No, the sneaky little hussies had mated before coming to Thelma's house, and it seems female geckos and other lizards can hold sperm in their bodies for up to eighteen months. Non-addicted owners don't usually try to hatch the eggs because it's a complicated process that often ends with the mother geckos eating their young. But Thelma, of course, had to purchase an incubator, special containers, and hatching materials, while undergoing intensive training from the reptile specialists (curses on their heads!) at the store on lizard midwifery and infant gecko care.

Every time I visited during the gestational period, I'd get a tour of all the terrariums — the numbers seemed to increase each time — and a close look at the chalky white oval eggs nestled in their special bedding, and more information about their humidity and temperature requirements. I've no idea how the little monsters manage to reproduce in the wild.

I hoped the excitement of waiting for eggs to hatch would be enough to keep her stabilized, but no, Thelma went back to the reptile store. Like insidious pushers everywhere, the staff just had to introduce her to new varieties of lizards. She went in for gecko feeders (live worms to store in the refrigerator, yum), but was taken to see cages with bearded dragons. "Beardies" are much bigger, resembling tiny dinosaurs, and their lower jaw skin puffs out and turns black when they are angry or "in the mood for dragon love." Thelma was enthralled but able to resist adding to her menagerie. Did the lizard pusher take no for an answer and stop? Oh no, he opened a special cage, removed the dragon and put it in her hands while whispering the magic words — rescued, desperately needs a good home, greatly reduced price.

Somehow pushers seem to smell weakness. How did he know Thelma grew up in a household full of rescue kittens? How did he know she couldn't resist an animal in need? The rescue price was very low, but since beardies differ greatly from geckos, it cost her a bundle for all the supplies. And now the store knew how to work on her. Zeus, the first dragon rescue, was soon followed by Kronos. Those two, both males, were joined by Toad, a plump, pretty red girl who'd lost part of her tail, leaving a stump about half the normal length. I think the store staff had Thelma's phone on speed-dial for whenever they needed to sell stuff. All it took to guarantee a big sale was a rescued dragon to put in her hands.

And then it happened again — eggs! Toad laid twenty-seven fertile eggs, which meant another trip to buy a second incubator. Geckos lay two eggs at a time and will repeat the process up to six times a few weeks apart during breeding season. Beardies lay about twenty-five eggs in a clutch (cats and dogs have litters, lizards have clutches), which can mean a hundred eggs per season, per bearded dragon. Those eggs put Thelma on such a high every single time she looked at them, especially after she learned how to candle eggs and saw the little lizard babies moving inside. Thelma was hooked and would never be the same.

That's how Thelma's addiction started, but she's much worse now. There are cages in almost every room of her house. She has three incubators full of eggs and a chart identifying the parents of each clutch and the date they were laid. All her supplies come from wholesalers online because the reptile store doesn't stock enough. She even has big bins in her house where she raises her own worms and roaches — that's right, my lovely daughter is proud to have colonies of roaches in her home.

Thelma is still a pushover for rescue too. She has a five-foot-long iguana that sleeps in bed with one of her teenage sons and steals his favorite soft pillow. Karma, the iguana, is a diva that runs down the hallway to the bathroom and scratches on the side of the tub when she wants her daily bath. Neesa, a two-and-a-half foot savannah monitor, is also a rescue that loves to cuddle on Thelma's lap in soft blankets, and watch tv. Neesa can often be found sleeping stuck part-way under furniture since she thinks her body will follow wherever she sticks her head. A body that looks like a soft, leather-covered balloon will not fit the same space as a slender, snake-like head.

Heaven, for someone with LLS or RCD, is a reptile show. These events are fascinating for the public, fun for social lizard dabblers, and mesmerizing for addicts. Thelma never misses one within fifty miles of her home. Keeping her collection impulses under control at a show is a real challenge for her sons and me. During the last one Thelma stopped at an exhibit of poison frogs, mesmerized by the brilliant colors. The boys kept telling her she did not need to add poison frogs to the household, but we could see she was tuning them out. When she asked about care and pricing, I looked at the boys in horror. They nodded and disappeared into the crowd behind us. In minutes they came running back, then grabbed Thelma's arms from either side.

"Mom, you've got to see this. We just saw a huge, bright blue, veiled chameleon two rows over. He's so cool, and he's a rescue. The woman showing him says he's missing part of his tail because of an accident, so he needs a special home. And she's selling him and his enclosure for only $100!"

That did it. Frog forgotten, Thelma took off with the boys at a run. When I caught up, she looked so sad standing in front of an empty booth. "He's gone," she said. "Somebody else must have gotten him."

The boys grinned at me, then guided Thelma towards the frozen and freeze-dried rodents for sale nearby, next to a huge display of snakes. They knew their mom liked looking at the beautiful patterns, but wouldn't want to buy one because of the feeding habits.

Lord only knows what will join the group next. Addiction is expensive, which is why Thelma stepped over a major line and became a wholesale dealer herself. At least she only sells to wholesalers, rather than trying to hook new lizard addicts. I tell myself that since she doesn't keep all the babies and the boys are helping to prevent her from branching out into other species, she isn't in danger of progressing from LLS to full blown RCD, but perhaps I'm grasping at straws.

I can't help my daughter, but perhaps sharing our experience can help prevent other people from developing the same addiction. If you think you have a family member who might be headed toward LLS, here is a checklist of symptoms to watch for:

1. Do they have multiple lizards, often multiple types as well?
2. Do they keep adding to their collection?
3. Do they spend hours on social media chatting about lizards?
4. Do they constantly take pictures and videos of their lizards and share them on social media?
5. Do they have hundreds more lizard pictures on their phones than family photos?
6. Do they know more about lizard genetics and their pet's genealogy than they do about their family?
7. Do they always use the word "reptile," never "lizard?"

Wait a minute. I don't have a single reptile, but I have lots of pictures of them on my phone and shared posts on my Facebook page. I've learned a lot about reptile care and feeding and often give pointers to new owners. When I go to Thelma's place I always hold and pet them, even though it's like petting a cross between a cactus and a steel wool pad. I think reptile babies are cute, even when they have their little mouths open ready to bite. One of my favorite new shows is *Scaled*. I always record it so I never miss an episode.

Oh my god, can you get LLS from secondary exposure like smoking?

OH NO — HELP, I NEED AN INTERVENTION!

Sharon Darrow is an entrepreneur, business owner, award winning author, public speaker, and an expert in caring for neonatal orphan kittens. Two of her books are about animal rescue, *Bottlekatz, A Complete Care Guide for Orphan Kittens* and *Faces of Rescue, Cats, Kittens and Great Danes*. Two are inspirational, a memoir titled *Hindsight to Insight, A Traditional to Metaphysical Memoir* and *Tom Flynn, Medium & Healer*. Her fifth non-fiction is a training manual about publishing, *Navigating the Publishing Maze, Self-Publishing 101*. She also writes historical fiction. *She Survives*, is the first in a four book series, inspired by her maternal grandmother. The second book of the series, *Strive and Protect*, was released June 1, 2019. Sharon firmly believes that life just gets better and richer, the longer you live. Her personal motto is "Find harmony within, then all things are possible."

THE FRENCHMAN AND HIS WOLF

T.A. BRANDON

Colorado mountains, near Ouray 1840

A white wolf, brushed with black and silver on the tips of his fur, trotted out of the pines and up onto the craggy mountain. He'd hunted all day and caught nothing to fill his hungry belly. He raised his snout to the sky, opened his jaws and howled his agony to the surrounding forest.

It was a heartfelt, soulful cry, but no one answered. He'd not expected one. He'd been traveling for days and had no contact with others of his kind. It was as if they had all disappeared, right along with his prey.

The only living thing he'd encountered was a big, French mountain man who was hunting game for their furs. The pelts were tied onto the back of the trapper's pack mule. Wolf was curious about the hunter, but made sure the man didn't catch sight of him.

The man's camp had the smell of meat, drawing Wolf's attention. Maybe he could sneak some scraps from the man somehow. He sat in the woods and watched from afar as the trapper ate his fill of meat and threw the remains into the woods away from his fire. Wolf would wait until after sunset, to quietly slip into the area where the scraps and bones were lying, to devour them.

Big fluffy snowflakes fell throughout the night, blanketing the brown muddy ground in pristine white. Wolf woke cocooned in a snowdrift, only his head above the white powdery stuff. He stood and shook his coat free of the snow. Hunting alone, without a wolf pack, meant he had to look for small prey. It would be even harder to hunt in the snow because they'd be hidden beneath the thick layer of snow. If he found no prey, he might have to follow the trapper and hope for scraps again.

Wolf decided to go up the nearby hill to hunt for anything hiding in the crevices and caves in the cliffs above. He followed the pungent scent of something he'd never before come across.

When he approached the entrance to a cave, he heard movement and a scraping of claws on the stone floor. The hair on his back bristled. He knew he was in danger, but he was too close to turn and run. He stood his ground, lips snarling, large canines bared, waiting to see what emerged and hoping he could fight it without being torn to bits. Whatever was in there sounded huge.

Suddenly, the biggest creature Wolf had ever seen came hurling out of the dark cave, growling its outrage. The grizzly lumbered toward him and swung its huge paw, cuffing Wolf so hard it knocked him onto the steep edge of the overhang. The snow beneath him gave way and Wolf slid off the cliff, dropping far below. His last thought was how much pain he was in before he slipped into darkness.

*　*　*

When Louis, the French trapper, crawled out of his makeshift tent the next morning, he smiled at the beautiful mantle of snow that covered the forest and beyond. It was a wondrous sight, but the snow could become dangerous if it got any deeper. He stretched, then gathered wood to start a fire for his camp coffee and chewed on some leftover venison jerky.

Louis decided to hunt for game near the cliffs above the nearby hill. He could check for a cave at the same time, in case there was a blizzard and he needed more shelter than his flimsy make-do tent.

He'd seen wolf tracks around his camp the past few days and wondered if the animal was stalking him. There only seemed to be one set of tracks though, so at least it was no wolf pack.

Louis hadn't traveled far, when he spotted what looked like a German shepherd lying in the snow just beneath the overhanging rock face. As he got closer, he saw that it wasn't a dog. Nope. By Golly, it was a young wolf. Figuring it was dead, Louis planned to take its fur, but when he reached down and lifted the animal's head, it opened its eyes and tried to snarl.

Louis jumped back, but the wolf didn't move. He wasn't sure how the wolf had gotten hurt. It only had a couple of smears of blood on its side. But Louis was struck by the idea that it looked so much like the dog he'd had as a kid that he couldn't bring himself to end its life just for fur.

He decided that he'd make camp here and see what happened. He'd seen rabbit tracks nearby and decided to follow the tracks to see if he could find the little critter for supper.

Louis shot the rabbit, then built a fire to cook it. When he'd eaten his fill, he looked over at the still unmoving wolf on the other side of the fire. He took the leftovers and laid them beside the wolf's mouth and stepped away. The wolf wiggled his noise at the scent and opened his still pain-glazed eyes to sniff the meat.

Louis returned to his side of the campfire and watched as the wolf slowly raised his head and began to ravenously devour the food, bones and all. He struggled to get up, but collapsed back to the ground and lay still, staring across at the trapper. Before he went to bed, Louis melted some snow in a small pot and set it beside the wolf's sleeping head.

When Louis woke the next morning, the wolf was gone. He was glad the animal was well enough to take off. Louis packed up and started his hunt for the day, but each evening, after cooking himself something to eat, he observed the wolf trotting back and forth in the tree line watching his camp. And each time, he threw the remains of his meal toward the skinny wolf.

Even when Louis was traveling and hunting from place to place, he noticed the wolf trailing behind. Little by little, the wolf came closer to the camp, until eventually he made himself comfortable across the fire from Louis. Just to pass the time, Louis began talking to the wolf as if he could actually understand what was being said. They made an uneasy peace.

* * *

Wolf trailed after the mountain man who had begun to hunt above the rocky outcroppings where Wolf had fallen off the cliff. The trapper was following an animal trail worn through the pines, when unexpectedly his horse and pack mule began acting nervously and pulling on their reins.

All of a sudden, a grizzly came roaring out of the thick brush beside the trail. The huge bear stood up on his hind legs and swiped its claws across the loaded pack on the mule, knocking the camp-gear onto the ground. The mule jerked his head back and forth as he twisted around, hee-hawing in panic. The raging bear tried to grab the mule's flank, but ended up ripping the furs from its pack instead. The mule's tether finally broke free and he raced off.

The mountain man was trying to control his horse and aim his rifle, but the terrified horse kept swinging its rear from one side to the other to evade the bear's grasp. The man fought valiantly to stay in his saddle but dropped his rifle.

Managing to pull out a large hunting knife, he reached out and swung hard at the bear's head. When the bear's ear came off and fell to the ground, the animal roared and lunged for the man's horse, but his horse jerked around again. The bear's claws missed the horse, but scraped deeply across the man's leg, almost unseating him.

Wolf attacked the bear from behind, snarling and biting at the bear's flanks. The distraction allowed the trapper to escape on his horse as the grizzly turned toward Wolf. The bear's clenching jaws snapped violently closed, narrowly missing him. Wolf raced into the forest, knowing that both the trapper and he had just escaped death.

When Wolf looked back, he saw the enraged bear swiping his paw at the place on his head where his ear had been. Blood streamed off the bear's head and splattered all over the ground, atop the scattered camp dishes and animal pelts. Wolf turned and hurried after the trapper.

* * *

Louis's leg hurt like hell and left a cherry red trail of blood in the snow, which he hoped the bear would not pursue. He was too weak to fight the bear off and had lost his rifle in the ruckus. The mountain man hastily wrapped his bandana around his wounded leg and pressed down to stem the blood flow. Louis hoped to make it to the Indian camp where he traded. It wasn't too far away. Once there, the Indians could tend to his leg and trade him another rifle. The Frenchman was surprised to look back and see the wolf trailing him.

When Louis rode into camp with his bloody leg, one of the Cheyenne traders helped Louis down from his horse.

"What happened?" Eagle Hunter asked.

In stilted Cheyenne, Louis replied, "Grizzly attack."

Another Cheyenne, Two Feathers, helped Louis across the snow-covered ground and underneath a makeshift shelter. He cleaned and bandaged Louis' leg.

Eagle Hunter returned to Louis with a dish of food.

"Here, must eat," he said, as he looked warily at the lone wolf staying just on the edge of their camp, and whose eyes remained on Louis.

"Thanks," Louis said, as he managed to sit up and reach for the food.

When Louis finished eating, Two Feathers took his dish and said, "Need warm place to sleep. You stay with Two Feathers."

The Frenchman woke at daybreak and rose wearily to his feet. Many of the Cheyenne were still asleep. *Damn, there wouldn't be any coffee this morning.* Louis wished the Indians drank the stuff. His leg hurt like hell, and without his coffee, he was going to be as grouchy as that bear who attacked him.

Louis looked around for Eagle Hunter to trade an extra

knife for a rifle. Once the negotiations were done, Louis pulled his gloves from his saddlebags and was about to mount up when Two Feathers put his hand on Louis' shoulder and stopped him.

"Mountain Man not go. Leg bleed again, not good."

Louis insisted on leaving. "I left my camp gear sprawled all over creation and I need to try to find my pack mule," he said, hoping they understood some of what he was saying. He wanted to be on his way.

Eagle Hunter handed Louis a handful of jerky and watched as Louis heaved himself up and onto his horse.

Both of the Cheyenne watched as the wolf came out of his hiding place and loped after the mountain man. But none of them saw the grizzly…

* * *

Two trappers out hunting happened to stumble onto the camp gear and animal pelts scattered over the ground, including the sliced off ear of a bear. Peering down at the bear's ear and how much blood lay splattered all over everything, the older trapper said, "Looks to me like whoever tangled with that bear must have been killed. Otherwise, whoever it was wouldn't have left their camp gear and that pile of furs."

"I bet you're right," the younger man said. "Those furs could make us a load of money. Let's load 'em up and add 'em to our own."

"Okay, you get the furs and I'll snag the camp gear. Bring your pack mule over here and start packin' him up. I wanna get outta here fast. I don't want no angry grizzly to come back and attack us."

When the trappers stopped by the Indian camp to trade later that day, they heard bits and pieces of a story about a Frenchman and his wolf. Unable to communicate with the Indians too well, they traded some of the camp gear they'd found and then headed out.

"I couldn't figure out what that Injun was saying most 'a

the time," the older man said.

"Me neither," the younger trapper replied. "I couldn't tell whether they heard the bear had killed the Frenchman after he left the Indian camp, or that they heard about him being attacked by the bear before the Frenchman even came to the Cheyenne camp."

"But, I'm pretty sure it was his gear that we scavenged," said the older man.

As the hunters left the Cheyenne camp, they turned to go farther up the mountain. They didn't notice the big grizzly stand up on his hind paws and sniff the air as he watched the two trappers and their mules start up the hill.

* * *

The Frenchman and his wolf were never again seen in the small town at the bottom of the mountain, or by any of the Indians at the Cheyenne camp. And neither were the two trappers.

But for years afterward, there were rumors of a one-eared grizzly stalking mountain men. And more than one trapper claimed that a large helpful Frenchman, accompanied by a white wolf tipped in black and silver, had saved their lives when they'd gotten hurt and were unable to take care of themselves.

Tales spread that a ghost roamed those mountains, helping injured hunters. No one ever seemed to learn the mountain man's name, but remembered he spoke broken English with a French accent. And they always described the white wolf with the black and silver tipped fur that followed him wherever he went.

The townspeople in Ouray, Colorado refer to the rare sightings of the Frenchman and his wolf as the Legend of the Mountain.

Tammy wanted to be a writer since she was 15, and that was a long time ago. Her first career started as a dispatcher. Then, when women were permitted to become officers, she became a cop. She found it a colorful and interesting lifestyle and has many tales to tell about it.

In her next career she became a day-spa owner, where she was licensed as a massage therapist, aesthetician, manicurist, and hypnotherapist. She had a quaint and beautiful little shop and treated her customers with the finest of care and service.

Now she has begun a new journey to finally fulfill her life-long dream of being an author. Although she's mostly published short stories thus far, she is a prolific writer and is currently working on more than one novel to be published in the future. Writing is one of the things she loves most, besides doo-wop music and dancing the tango. You can find her at TABrandon.com.

PIGARO, PIGARO, PIGARO

DUNCAN MACVEAN, D.V.M.

Petunia, a perky pot-bellied pig, lived with her "Dad" in an upstairs apartment in Sacramento near the California State Capitol building. Every morning Dad Tim put her in a harness with a dog leash – every morning except on days he was on stage at the San Francisco Opera House booming forth his melodious baritone voice.

Tim did not look like the prototypical opera singer. No barrel chest, not short, and no beard. He was over six feet tall and skinny. Whenever I saw him, he wore a tight T-shirt and khaki shorts, exposing his protruding ribs and match-stick legs.

Petunia stood about two feet tall, barely reaching Tim's mid-shins. The two of them, tall rail-like Tim and tiny Petunia, made quite an unusual pair as he walked her like a dog along the sidewalks of downtown Sacramento. Tim even carried plastic bags to scoop up Petunia's poop.

I met Petunia and Tim on a gorgeous blue-sky day in spring. I parked my car in a small paved lot next door to the apartment building. The sign read "Resident Parking Only." I hoped Tim had a placard I could place on the dashboard so my car wouldn't be towed away, but, just in case, I taped my business card to the driver-side window, hoping any parking-ticket agent might conclude that I was there to see a patient on a veterinary house call.

The lower level of the building was a small mom-and-pop market. There was a door leading up to the apartments to the left of the front, street side, of the store. The entrance to Tim's pad was on the parking side of the building. The stairs up to his apartment were wooden steps with a steel railing that led up to a small landing at his doorstep. As I climbed the stairway lugging my medical bag, I wondered if he had to carry his pig up and down the stairs on his comings and goings. That question was answered momentarily.

I heard someone from down below call my name as I ascended the stairs. There was Tim with Petunia in tow strolling along the sidewalk. He waved and said, "Wait at the top. The door is locked." He gave a little whistle as he reached the bottom of the stairs, and Petunia immediately started bounding her way up the steps. *Clearly, no need to carry that little girl.* Later, when I started in on a mini-lecture regarding how descending stairs could be rough on a pig's shoulder, knee and ankle joints, Tim assured me he always carried 'Tunia down the steps. He also mentioned that they were moving to an apartment that was on the ground floor. He added, "The new apartment has a small backyard, so 'Tunia can root outside sometimes instead of tossing our rugs all over the place."

Tim unlocked the wooden door that was painted a subdued violet color. He ushered me in as Petunia chuffed at my pant legs. The apartment was artfully decorated. Colorful throw rugs on dark walnut flooring, quilts over the dark leather couch and easy chair, reproductions of Miro and Picasso paintings hung on a wall, a multi-hued stained-glass lampshade covered the lights over a knotty pine dinner table.

An aroma of lemon filled the air, as if the table had been rubbed with citrus oil. Rich-textured curtains hung at the exits to a hallway and to the kitchen off the main room. Overhead lighting was recessed with spotlights aimed at the paintings. One of the spotlights highlighted a high-end record player and stereo speakers on a cream-colored cabinet against one wall. The room was well lit by windows at the back of the main room. It all was strikingly memorable to me. It was a living space of comfort, and I asked about it.

"Ah, yes. The decorative touches are my partner John's tasteful doings. The music is mine." Then he proceeded to tell me he was a lead baritone for the San Francisco Opera. John, he said, was a chef at one of the restaurants in downtown Sacramento. They also had an apartment in the Castro district of San Francisco. Tim would stay there when he had continual work at the Opera, and John would take care of Petunia while he was gone.

Dishes rattled behind the curtain to the kitchen. I set my bag down on a chair next to the table and pointed towards the noise of pottery clinking. "I guess that's John getting a meal together."

"No, it's 'Tunia rooting among her water and food bowls, looking for a drink and snack. But they're empty since you told me not to feed or water her this morning. I'll go get her." And off he went, parting the drapes hanging at the archway to the kitchen.

I pulled out the smallest of my hoof nippers, blood-clotting powder, syringes with needles, bottles of sedative and reversing agent, and vaccine vials, and arranged them on the floor in a well-lit area near the windows.

Petunia ambled out of the kitchen, reluctantly moving ahead of Tim's herding motions. She let out a little squeal. I supposed she was disappointed at no morsel in her dish. Her harness had been removed. She made a beeline for my bag and stood up on her hind legs with front legs on the chair edge. She sniffed my bag and shoved it with her snout.

"Ha, Tim, I think she discovered with that good smeller of hers that I have pet treats in my bag." I got down on my knees and put my arms around her. As I did so, I noticed a hint of lavender. "She sure smells good. I like the touch of lavender."

"We bathed her yesterday." And with a smile he added, "Just for you!"

"Really. Many pigs hate bathing."

"'Tunia actually looks forward to it. We just walk her into the shower and lather her up with baby shampoo to which we've added a couple drops of lavender oil."

"That's a new one on me."

Still on the floor on my knees, I lifted Petunia to get some idea of her weight. *Uh, uh, heavy little thing! Around 50 pounds.* Little pot-bellies may be short, but they are compact and usually weigh more than a dog of comparable height. I lifted her lip and saw that her tusks were no longer than the rest of her teeth. *No need for a tusk trim.* I didn't really expect that she would since she was young, just over two years, and female pigs are much less likely to require tusk trimming than males.

I leaned back a little, hugging her to my chest, and rubbed her belly. She didn't seem to mind the restraint and appeared to like the tummy touch. Also, I took a good look at her hooves. "Well, Tim, there is not a lot to take off her toenails. Probably because they are worn by all those walks on concrete." Then I took hold of one of her front legs. She immediately squealed and struggled to get out of my hold. I let her go. She ran a few steps away from me and turned her head with her eyelids and forehead wrinkled up into a scowl.

"She does not like her feet touched. I can do most anything to her, but her feet are definitely off limits."

With a sigh, I replied, "I know. That's often the case with pigs unless they're trained to accept it at an early age. I'll give her a light sedative injection, so we can get the trimming done."

"A drug overture won't be necessary, Doc. I can make sure she's quite docile for your procedure."

"And how might that be?'

Tim ambled over to the stereo turntable, lifted the tone arm and gently placed the stylus on the black vinyl of a record. Melodic symphonic music began to flood the room. He winked at me and took in a deep breath. His thin chest expanded like the ribs of an accordion. What came out of his mouth were rich lofty tones of a lush aria from a Rossini composition. The vocal music filled the air. I was stunned at his modulating control from stirring softness to expansive explosion of sound settling into the quiet of a lake smooth as a mirror. Calm, soothing.

Then I heard a thud. Petunia had plopped over on her side halfway onto her back with legs straight out in front of her. Her eyelids fluttered and closed. She was out like a light.

She was in a hypnotic state. *Tim's singing! She responds with slumber as if she were a baby listening to a lullaby.*

No problemo. Trimming her hooves was a piece of cake. I

came close to the quick of one of her nails, and she didn't even flinch. It was easy giving her the once over examination and the vaccine shots.

As soon as I was through with the vet work, I stood up. "I'm done. That was the easiest pedicure I've ever given to a pig."

Tim ended the aria on a long base note. Within not even a minute of the end of his singing, Petunia stirred. Her curly eyelashes fluttered. She rolled over and stood up. She shook her body a couple of times like a wet dog after a shower. Getting her bearings, as if nothing unusual had happened, she deftly tiptoed over to sniff my bag again.

Oh, okay. I unzipped my bag, took out a vitamin dog treat and handed it to her. She crumbled it in her mouth and leisurely gulped a couple of times and then pointed her snout at my bag as if she were Charles Dickens's Oliver saying, "More, Sir."

Tim and I chuckled. He said he would have her favorite treat available for my next visit.

When I got down to the bottom of the steps and saw my car, I realized I'd forgotten to get the temporary parking permit from Tim. I was pleased to see my car had not been towed. I looked at the car's front window. No ticket under the windshield wiper. *Whew, I got away with it again. Who polices these parking spots anyway?*

I felt cheerful, looking forward to hearing more opera and a snoring pig in the future.

Duncan MacVean, D.V.M., was a professor of veterinary medicine at various universities and has published in peer-review journals. He has also worked with wild animals in Southeast Asian jungles and as a consultant for the Malaysian National Zoo and The Brookfield Zoo in

Chicago. Dr. MacVean "retired" back to his hometown of Sacramento, California, and has been a house-call veterinarian there for the past twenty-seven years. His memoir, *My Patients Like Treats: Tales from a House-Call Veterinarian*, was published in May 2018 by Skyhorse Publishing.

A LITTLE SUGAR AND SOME TLC

DÄNNA WILBERG

We had already buried two guinea pigs, two cats, and two betta fish when my daughter, Erika, begged me to babysit a litter of newborn kittens she acquired, unintentionally, at work. A tenant, in the apartment complex she managed, threatened to drown the kittens if they weren't removed from under her staircase. Erika explained how she had spent the day looking for the feral mother to no avail and how she couldn't take the kittens home with her because she was leaving for Hawaii the next day. "Please, Mom—you're my only hope," she said.

When she arrived with the five kittens, she brought everything needed for their care. Eyedroppers, special formula, and a little bed for them to snuggle in. I had to admit they were darling, and I could understand why she felt compelled to save them from their demise. But it wasn't until they were with me for a couple of days that I realized they were in distress.

The kittens all became lethargic and wouldn't eat. They whimpered a lot. Their eyes, barely open, became weepy, and their tiny noses, runny. I didn't know what to do, so I took them to the vet. The vet diagnosed them with conjunctivitis, prescribed ointment for their eyes, and said if they didn't improve in 24 hours to come back for tests.

Within 24 hours, their condition worsened. I sought out another vet, hoping to get a better prognosis, but that vet's attitude was similar to the first. The vet prescribed antibiotics, but said that most likely the kittens contracted a virus, and there wasn't much that could be done. It seemed no one wanted to help these tiny creatures.

My oldest daughter, Ashleigh, and I cared for the kittens as best we could. We administered the ointment and antibiotics, but their condition worsened and soon, we were out of options. The inflammation in their eyes caused such swelling that their eyeballs popped out of the sockets. It was pitiful to watch them suffer, and I felt we were doing them a disservice trying to keep them alive. It was time to put them down.

Disappointed with the reception we received from the vets in our immediate area, Ashleigh and I took the litter to a local cat clinic. The vet took one look at the kittens and immediately quarantined the area. She agreed they were far beyond saving, and most likely had FHV, feline herpesvirus. Letting them go was the only humane thing to do.

As the vet began preparing the injections, we held each one and said our goodbyes. It was then Ashleigh noticed one blue eye looking up at her. "Can this one be saved?" she asked the vet, tears ready to spill.

"I can give her more antibiotics," the vet said, "but her chances are very grim. And even if she does survive, her quality of life is going to be compromised. Being so little, and having just one eye, she may not be able to find her balance—and then there are her respiratory issues. She can't be let around other cats either, or she will spread the disease."

"We have to try, Mom." There was no convincing my daughter otherwise.

We took the kitten home, our hopes beginning all over again. Because the kitten's two white paws, white chest, and chin made her look like she was dipped in white powder, Ashleigh named her Sugar.

The next few weeks were touch and go. I took Sugar with me to a healing class I was attending at the time. Four amazing healers laid hands on her and we prayed for her recovery. Each day Sugar got stronger and stronger. The vet was right, she had balance issues. When she first started walking, she'd fall over on her side. I began working with her; using a rod with feathers on the end, I moved it from side to side, directing her focus left and right. This exercise helped her brain develop equally on both sides, and eventually, her balance improved. I also did energy work on her, and prayed. Within a few weeks, we not only noticed immense improvement, we also realized a miracle was occurring. Sugar's empty eye socket was filling up with fluid. A couple of weeks later, the swollen lid opened to reveal an eye. It was slightly turned and the cornea dull, but it seemed as though she could see just fine.

Needless to say, the vet was amazed at Sugar's progress, and agreed she was a miracle in many ways. (Sugar's photo was pinned to the bulletin board in the Cat Clinic reception area and remained there for many years.)

Once Sugar began acting like any normal tot, she displayed curiosity for the outdoors. As a precaution, we bought her a harness and restricted her to the patio. It wasn't long before she longed to explore the open hills behind our house and howled until she got her way. The young, spunky feline crept through the tall weeds, tethered to a leash, but happy all-the-same.

After years of leash training, we decided to let Sugar out on her own. She was very good about staying nearby, and any cat coming in close proximity was chased away. She hissed at everyone who came near her, with the exception of my husband, and I was convinced being territorial was due to being raised without siblings. Then again, keeping her on a leash may have squelched her social skills, but the idea of her spreading her illness was always a concern.

In the last fifteen years, Sugar has grown to be one spoiled kitty. Shredding our leather furniture was the first sign that we had created a monster. My husband made her a fabulous scratching post with plush carpet and a tier for climbing, but she prefers the corners of the couch — especially when we're away, and can't keep to her stringent feeding schedule. And clip her nails? Try holding a Tasmanian devil! Our little miracle cat can puncture multiple parts of your body before you can blink.

Sugar is *very* smart. When she wants breakfast, she claws the carpet in the doorway to my bedroom. At exactly 7:00 PM, she appears out of nowhere, demanding her dinner. She will flop down at my feet, herd me through the house like a sheltie, or sit nearby and stare holes in my head. Lately, she's developed a new skill: howling. She's decided that sleeping past 8:00 A.M. is no longer an option. Once she is fed, she scratches at the door to be let out for her morning drink. Evidently the water outside in the planters and the bird dish tastes much better than fresh water from the faucet. The only way she'll drink the water inside is if I put three ice cubes in her dish. If I put two cubes in her dish, she gets insulted and will sit beside her dish until I add the third. If I put four, she walks away. I can almost hear her mumble, "Stupid human, can't you count?"

There are definite pitfalls to owning a spoiled, obnoxious, "delicate" cat, but then there are times when she is so in tune to my needs that I swear she's divine. When I am sick, she is by my side, projecting an unconditional love, both comforting and healing. When I am sad, she knows. She understands my pain, no words needed. The love and care she has been shown through the years has not gone unrewarded, it has been returned tenfold.

Dänna Wilberg is a novelist, an award-winning short film maker, and former TV host/producer from northern California.

Her romantic suspense trilogy, *The Red Chair*, *The Grey Door*, and *The Black Dress*, features Psychotherapist Grace Simms. Dänna is also published in several anthologies, including one in London.

Her current works in progress include a paranormal-suspense series based on her short film, *Borrowed Time*, featuring intuitive Suzanne Cash. Besides writing, Dänna is passionate about traveling, karaoke, killer cheesecake, and her wee ones.
Visit: dannawilberg.com.

THE RED FOX AND THE GREAT HORNED OWL

CHARLENE JOHNSON

A red fox lounged on the broad branch of a big-leaf maple tree, basking in the early morning summer sun. Still sated from the rabbit he caught during the night, he couldn't think of a better way to while away the hours until she appeared.

He sat at attention when the great horned owl emerged through the copse of trees; her magnificent wings stretched wide as she glided silently through the air, her sharp talons poised for attack if any unfortunate prey crossed her path.

For the last week the owl had hunted in the clearing, her attention focused on the massive trunk of a fallen redwood, a victim of the recent big wind storm that swept through the area a few years ago.

The fox knew the owl was female because she was much larger than other horned owls he'd seen, and female owls tended to be larger than their male counterparts.

A family of squirrels had taken up residence in a hollowed-out section of the fallen tree. The squirrels scampered in and out of the nest all day and night as they foraged for food. They gathered berries and seeds in the thick bushes and scurried up the tall trees to collect nuts.

There were times the owl would fly over the surrounding area, then perch on a nearby branch not far away and watch them, still as a statue. The only movement was the peculiar rotation of her head, which seemed to the fox to be otherworldly. On a few occasions, she flew down and sat on top of the tree trunk, waiting for one of the squirrels to surface from its nest. So far, the owl had been unsuccessful.

It amused the fox that the attempts to capture one of the frisky squirrels eluded the owl, a silent, deadly predator. She came back time and time again. He didn't know why she kept returning to the tree trunk and the squirrels. There was so much forest to hunt in. So many creatures to prey on.

He had to admit, he didn't mind seeing her every day. She was a beautiful bird with her mottled gray feathers and her reddish-brown face. There was a patch of white feathers that covered her throat. But it was the eyes that drew him in. When she rotated her head in his direction, her large penetrating yellow eyes with their prominent black pupils were expressionless but intriguing. They mesmerized him. And just as quickly, her head rotated back to the tree trunk.

Had the owl sensed he was watching her? He didn't know if it was him she was looking at, or if she was drawn by another sound in his direction. Did she know he was there? He wasn't well hidden in the tree that he had declared his own. It wasn't his intention to hide. He came upon the tree by chance a few months ago and decided it was where he wanted to spend his days when he was in this forest.

He wondered if the owl had young ones she needed to feed. That could account for her persistence, but her lack of success would not feed owlets. Where was her mate? Surely, he should be helping her.

A doe ran into the clearing, looking skittish. Something or someone was chasing it. Minutes later, he heard human voices shouting, and loud footsteps coming their way.

"I think the deer went this way. She can't have gotten far. Let's go."

The fox looked down from his perch and saw two hunters enter the clearing. They glanced eagerly around, rifles held at the ready in their hands.

"Which way did she go, Jock?"

The other hunter pointed east. "This way, I think."

As they started in that direction, the first hunter stopped. "Hey, Jock, check out that owl in the tree."

"Where, Steve?"

Steve inclined his head to the tree standing directly behind the fallen tree trunk. "Up there, staring right at us. It's creeping me out the way it stares. I've never liked those damned birds."

"Aren't they supposed to be the harbingers of death?"

"That's what my grandpa always said." Steve aimed his rifle at the owl and pulled the trigger.

The fox watched in horror as the owl collapsed on the tree branch and tried to grab it with her talons. She managed to hold on for a few seconds before losing her grip and wobbling off. The owl hit a branch on the way down, then another and another before finally falling to the forest floor with a thud.

"Why did you do that, Steve? Are you crazy?"

"I told you, I hate owls."

"Well, your stupidity may have just cursed us. I have enough bad luck without you adding to it. Let's get the hell out of here before something bad happens. I hear these woods are haunted."

The two hunters took off through the forest heading north, forgetting about the deer.

The fox, a bit stunned by what he'd just seen, leaped from his perch and jumped over the fallen tree trunk to the owl, who lay unmoving on a bed of pine needles. He nudged the owl with his nose, and she stirred, opening her captivating yellow eyes.

He started to move back in case she tried to attack him, but she didn't. She simply stared at him, a wavering cry the only sound she made. He surveyed her body, looking for where the bullet had struck her. He found a wound that was partially open and bleeding in her upper left wing. She needed immediate care.

The fox looked around before trotting behind the tree. A moment later, in the place of the fox was a naked man crouched on the ground. He stood up and went back to the owl. He bent over her and stroked her feathers gently.

"I'm going to get you some help."

The owl responded by emitting another wavering cry.

Dex Brooks strode around the fallen tree and removed a

pile of leaves from the base of his tree to uncover a small duffle bag. He opened it and took out a tee shirt, a pair of jeans, socks and tennis shoes. Dressing quickly, he picked up the duffle bag and returned to the owl.

He took a tea towel and wrapped the wound as best as he could. When through, Dex gently picked her up and placed her in the bag, leaving it open for her to breathe. He cradled the bag in his arms, not wanting to jostle her around to risk hurting her further, and headed south through the forest to where he had left his truck at a campground parking lot a mile away.

He drove into town to McHenry's Animal Clinic and was happy to see the clinic wasn't busy. He went to the reception desk and was immediately ushered into an examination room.

"Morning, Dex," Dr. McHenry greeted him as he entered the room. "What poor creature are you bringing in for treatment this time?"

Dex set his duffle bag down on the exam table, lifted the injured owl out and laid her on the table.

"A hunter shot her."

"I'll be damned," Dr. McHenry exclaimed. "That's something I don't see every day." He took the towel off and examined the wound. "The bullet went straight through. I'll need to take some x-rays. The wing might be fractured. I'm going to sedate her. It will make it easier on her."

Dex stood beside the exam table. The owl's eyes were fastened on him. He didn't know for sure, but his presence seemed to calm her. He reached out and stroked her head.

"I don't think you'll need to. She's fine."

"She seems to like you. I've never seen an owl so trusting."

"Our paths have crossed more than once. She's been going into the area in the forest I frequent."

"I'll take her into the X-ray room. I only need a couple of X-rays. You can wait for her in this room or the lobby."

"I'll wait here."

"She has a fracture," Dr. McHenry said a half hour later. "I'll tape the wing against her side to keep it in place. She'll be able to walk around and feed herself, but it'll take four to six weeks for it to heal enough for her to fly again. I assume you're taking her home with you?"

"I was planning to. At least until she can fly, then I'll take her back to the forest."

"I can let you borrow a large bird cage to use for her until she heals."

"That's not necessary."

* * *

Dex spread out some bed pads on the floor in his sunroom and got the owl settled. He thought she would be more comfortable there. On the way home he stopped at the grocery store and bought some ground beef for her to eat since hunting for prey was out of the question. She seemed content to eat the ground meat he left for her.

"I'm going to call you Sadie, after my favorite song by the Spinners," he told the owl the day after he brought her home. She whistled, and he thought she liked the name too.

After a few days, they settled into a comfortable routine. Dex was a graphic designer, did freelance work for publishing companies, magazines, and marketing firms, and made a good living. He had deadlines to meet, and at times, the work was grueling, but he was able to balance it with the need to shift. Being a shape-shifter, he could shift into any mammal, reptile or bird he wished. Of late, his preference was the red fox.

Working from home made it possible for Dex to spend time with Sadie. As she began to heal, the owl would perch on the edge of his drafting table and watch him work. He would talk to her as if she were human, and every evening she would sit on the couch beside him and watch TV.

At night, he would read *Guardians of Ga'Hoole* to her before turning in for the night. There were thirty-one books in the series, and she would be healed way before they got through all thirty-one.

The closer it got to the day Dex would have to set the owl free, the more anxious he became. On those days when he had to go out for a few hours, getting back home to see her became something he looked forward to.

She's an owl, Dex, he told himself. *She's not a shape-shifter like you. You can't keep her. She needs to be in the forest. It's where she belongs.*

If he was willing to give up being human, he could shift into a horned owl and be her mate – if she didn't already have one in the forest waiting for her.

"I wish you could talk to me. I have so many questions to ask that you can't answer. I haven't spent this much time with anyone in a very long time. It's good to have someone to come home to. It's been hard for me to get close to anyone because of the dual life I live. My parents died years ago, and I have no living relatives that I know of. Soon, you will be well enough to be set free. I have to admit, I will miss you."

Sadie sat on the arm of the couch and regarded him with her hypnotic eyes.

Dex sighed and headed for the kitchen to pour a cup of coffee. He sat down at the kitchen counter and took a sip of the strong dark coffee, staring out the French doors that led to the back yard. A sudden realization filled him. He had bonded with the enchanting owl, and when she was back in the forest, she would fly away, and he would never see her again. She would go back to her life as an owl, and he would have to learn to live with it. Dex would never again be able to go to that spot in the forest and not think about her. Regrettably, he would have to find another spot to call his own.

"I saw you shift into your fox one evening, you know. I thought you were the most handsome man I'd ever seen. That's why I kept coming back to the clearing. The squirrels were only my excuse. I came back there for you."

Dex's coffee cup clattered to the counter, coffee splashing across the granite tile. He whirled around to look at her. "You're a shifter, just like me!"

"Yes, I am."

Dex was completely blown away by the beautiful woman standing before him with the throw blanket from his couch tucked around her, like a towel after a shower. She had toffee brown skin and hazel eyes with flecks of gold. Her hair was a mass of black curls that hung below her shoulders. He couldn't have dreamed up a more perfect woman.

"What is your name?"

"It's Felicity. Felicity Singleton."

Dex got up from the kitchen counter and took her hands in his. He smiled broadly, feeling true happiness for the first time in his life. It was rare to find another of his kind. Most wanted anonymity, and chose to hide what they were.

"Felicity, does that mean I don't have to take you back to the forest and free you?"

She smiled impishly back at him. "No, Dex. You never have to."

"You must have a home. Someone has to be missing you."

Felicity's smile faltered. "No. I left home a long time ago. I haven't seen my family in years. I was the only shapeshifter in my family and kept my duality a secret. If I had told my parents what I was, they would have locked me in the loony bin."

Dex nodded. "Growing up in a strictly human family would be problematic. My parents and my siblings were shapeshifters and that was my normal. Being around humans has always been abnormal." He paused, pulling her into his arms. "I never thought I'd find someone like you."

"Me either, Dex."

"Where do we go from here?" he asked slowly, losing himself in her mesmerizing eyes.

A mischievous smile crossed her face. "How about a run in the forest?"

* * *

The red fox glided through the forest, in pursuit of the white fox with the hazel eyes. She stopped long enough for him to get close, then sped off again, a white blur against the earth-toned landscape.

He had never experienced such exhilaration. To have someone special to share his world with was more than the red fox could have ever hoped for. The white fox, forced to survive in the world on her own, had finally found a place to call home. Dex was her home.

After a playful hour of cat and mouse, the white fox stopped and hopped up on a low hanging branch of a gnarled California Live Oak, waiting for her red fox.

He silently leaped up beside her and rubbed his snout along the soft thick fur of her neck, luxuriating in the feel of her.

The white fox purred, preening in her mate's loving care, and when he was done, she did the same for him.

His deep, contented purrs filled the air.

As day turned into night, the foxes curled tenderly around one another and slept until dawn. The fox became Dex and Felicity's animal of choice, but neither forgot how fate had brought them together.

The red fox and the great horned owl, bound together by a tragic event, had become the soulmates each had longed for. Neither of them would ever be alone again.

Charlene Johnson lives in Sacramento, California. She is married and has a son, a daughter and four grandchildren. She graduated cum laude from Waynesburg College with a bachelor's degree in liberal arts.

Books have always been one of her greatest passions. She is an author with Kingston Publishing Company and has published three books so far in her paranormal romance series *Circle of the Red Scorpion*. She also has poetry published in the American Poetry Anthology and Forever and A Day - The National Library of Poetry.

Charlene's currently working on Book 5 in the series and Book

1 in a new romantic thriller series.

Besides reading and writing, she also enjoys photography, travel, music, and great movies. Her website address is www.circleoftheredscorpion@gmail.com.

BEAR IN OUR TENT. YIKES!

ELVA ANSON

Big brown bears coming out of hibernation in early spring, starving and desperate, will eat anything. Families living at the foot of the majestic Sierra Nevada mountains grow up hearing warnings and horror stories about vicious hungry bears breaking into cars to steal food and even attacking people. My family went camping many times. Nothing bad ever happened to us. We always remembered to put our extra food in a bag and tie it to a tree out of the reach of the bears.

In the early spring of 1957, Everett and I took our friends, Dan and Darlene, camping in Yosemite. We learned first-hand why hungry bears should be avoided.

Darlene and I grew up in Reedley, a small town a few hour's drive from Yosemite. We roomed together in college. After graduation, we took teaching jobs in San Diego where we met our sailors. After marriage, Everett and I returned to my hometown. Darlene and Dan returned to Dan's hometown in New Mexico. Neither Dan nor Everett had visited Yosemite, a place Darlene and I loved.

One day a letter arrived. I quickly tore open the envelope and read, "We would like to visit you in the early spring."

"Ev! Ev!" I called as I ran to find him. "Darlene and Dan are going to visit us! We can take them to Yosemite! We can go camping, and you guys can see the falls in the early spring. I'm sure Dave and Sylvia will let us borrow their tent."

I was still talking after I found Everett. "It will be so much fun!"

Dave and Sylvia let us borrow their small tent. Stakes, driven through loops at the corners of the tent, stabilized the pole in the center. We borrowed a couple of sleeping bags and bought a lot of food: hot dogs and buns, several kinds of chips, pickles and all that goes with cooking over a fire-pit. We had a pound of bacon and a dozen eggs for breakfast, and cinnamon rolls for dinner and breakfast.

Dan and Darlene arrived late the night before our trip. Nobody got up early the next morning. Everett and Dan managed to pack the tent, sleeping bags, several blankets, camping gear, and food into the car. We got started after a quick lunch.

Four-lane mountain highways didn't exist in 1957. Sharp curves were not uncommon. We joined a couple of cars at a water stop to cool the radiator of our 1946 Ford sedan. Fortunately, none of us got car sick. Anticipation and excitement increased as we got closer to the park.

"The bears should still be hibernating," I cautioned. "We brought a canvas bag to store our food tonight. It can be pulled up to a tree branch."

"See what a great wife I have," Ev said. "She has everything planned." Everyone laughed.

Reaching the gates to the park ended all thoughts about bears. Everyone focused on the Park Ranger's instructions and a map to camp grounds. Empty camp grounds gave us many choices for camping spots.

"Hey, look, Everett. There is a campsite with a fire-pit, and some camper left firewood for us. It has a picnic table and a barbeque pit." I couldn't believe we could be so lucky.

Everett pulled into the spot. "There is a perfect tree for tying up our food tonight. The first thing we have to do, before we lose the sun completely, is to put up the tent."

The tent looked like a big sack with an opening for the door. It had a floor attached to its sides. After we had successfully set up the tent, the guys dug a trench around it, in case of rain. Four sleeping bags filled the tent with just enough room for our food in a corner by the door.

"I put the food box on the table already," Darlene said. "I hope no bears are watching."

Our condiments were in a bag. The food for our weenie roast was in a box on top of the food for breakfast.

The thought of bears brought back old fears I had on camping trips with my parents. They usually fell asleep before I did. Every time I heard steps or the leaves hit the tent, I thought it might be a bear. We were not the only campers in the campground then. I hadn't seen any campers in this campground. We were alone. What if there are bears coming out of hibernation? I shivered just thinking about it.

Dan got a blazing fire going. Everett lit the lantern and put it on the table. My fears vanished with the darkness. We were all ready to roast our hot dogs. Condiments, Darlene's salt and pepper shakers and a jar of jam were in one bag. Marshmallows and chocolate bars were in another bag. All were easily accessible. We had forgotten all about starving bears.

We roasted hot dogs over hot coals on sticks we would later use to roast marshmallows. We spread mustard or catsup on the buns. Hot dogs had never tasted better.

We discovered we all had different levels of skill at roasting marshmallows. We laughed when beautifully roasted marshmallows burst into flames and slipped off the stick into the fire. We voted Dan the best marshmallow roaster.

"How about a game of Hearts?" Dan suggested as he pulled a deck of cards out of his pocket. We threw our roasting sticks in the fire, and put the left-over food in the box on the table.

We hadn't been playing long when turning up the flame on the lantern couldn't compete with the deepening forest darkness. Distant rumbling became louder and louder. Soon the roar was right over us, and the skies opened up. We all jumped up, someone grabbed the food box, and ran for the tent. Fortunately, Everett remembered to bring the lantern.

When we reached the tent, we were dripping wet. Dan said, "It's just too crowded."

The sound of rain battering the tent added to the uneasy feeling I had.

"It's pretty late. Why don't we all go to bed?" I suggested.

72

"That's a good idea," Darlene said. "I'm really tired, and we have all day tomorrow to see the park. The falls are beautiful this early in the spring."

We took off our coats and crawled into our sleeping bags, fully clothed. No one thought about the food we had carried in and tucked in the corner of the tent.

The sound of rain hitting our tent and the darkness of the night put me to sleep quickly. I slept so soundly, I didn't know when Everett rolled over into water that had seeped through a small hole in the side of the tent. He got up and went to the car to spend the rest of the night. He left without waking anybody.

In the darkest part of early morning, smelly heavy breathing woke me. Seconds later, the sound of heavy canvas being slashed, followed by a scream, brought me out of my sleeping bag. I realized the scream had come from Darlene who was lying next to me. I wondered if she was hurt. She had grabbed the tent pole to keep the tent from collapsing.

I felt a strong wave of claustrophobia, mixed with terror. Dan, Darlene and I were hanging onto the pole trying to keep the tent steady, but where was Everett?

"He got my arm," Darlene said, strangely calm.

It took a minute for me to realize Darlene was talking about a bear.

We listened to the bear, unimpressed by our screams, sniffing his way around the outside of the tent to locate the food. Fortunately, he had not tried to come through the tear he had made first. Where was Everett? Had he gone to the restroom in the night, and the bear got him? "Oh God, no!" I cried aloud. I hoped he had gone to the car and had locked himself in.

We could see nothing in the black darkness. We felt and smelled the movement of the bear. He smelled like a garbage dump. He located the food with his nose and let out a satisfied snort as he slashed the side of the tent for the second time with his big paw. I wondered how we could ever pay for the tent.

The bear slowly came in through the front door. Inside the

tent, he smelled like a skunk. He settled down noisily in front of the food box while he consumed all of the bacon, eggs, and cinnamon rolls, along with their plastic containers. He left nothing but the large empty cardboard box.

The big bear filled a third of the tent. Dan's whispered voice sounded worried. "We are in a sack with a stinky hungry bear, and there's no way to get out."

"What can we do?" I whispered back.

"Can't you girls scream louder?" It frightened me to know Dan was scared, too.

The three of us desperately clung to the wobbly tent pole. We all knew our carelessness with the food brought the bear to our tent.

Suddenly, lights dimly lit the tent. My first thought was relief. Everett must have turned on the car headlights. He must be okay. Thank God, he was safe so far. Now, we could see how big this filthy bear was. He gave a long, satisfied belch and tried to stand, backing up toward the door.

I couldn't tell if the bear was shaking the pole or if we were shaking it. He looked at us, yawned and turned toward the door, dangerously shaking the sides of the tent as we held on tight to the tent pole. He sat half in and halfway out of the doorway.

We heard Everett's voice. "Go away, bear! Go away, bear!"

The bear growled. Everett must have come closer because the bear was now on all fours. He continued to growl. Slowly, he stood up on his two back feet and let out a roar. It shook the ground.

We heard feet running. A car door opened and closed with a bang. I hoped Everett was okay. It became eerily quiet. I thought I heard the bear moving slowly.

We let minutes go by before letting go of the tent pole, and cautiously looked out the door. The bear was slowly walking back into the dark forest with our condiment bag hanging from his mouth. Where had the bag been when he left the tent? Did he pick it up outside the tent when he headed into the woods?

"Oh no!" Darlene was upset. "The jar of jam and my salt

and pepper shakers are in that bag!"

The three of us grabbed some blankets. We joined Everett and spent the rest of the night in the car with the doors locked. We all had a story to tell for the rest of our lives. Darlene says she shows her first graders the scar on her arm when she tells the bear story. They are always impressed.

Elva Anson, a marriage family therapist for nearly forty years and former elementary school teacher, has raised three children and written six books. A popular speaker, she speaks on everything from relationship to personal growth. She has been on more than 70 radio talk shows across the country and several local and national TV shows. She has written for many magazines including Readers Digest.

Elva's first three books, *How to Keep the Family That Prays Together from Falling Apart*, *The Complete Book of Home Management*, *How to Get Kids to Help at Home*, all published by Moody Press, Chicago, have sold between sixteen to twenty thousand copies. Her next book, *Becoming Soul Mates*, published by Emidra Publishing, is in its second printing. *Teddy*, a short memoir written for a friend, had limited sales.

Her sixth book, *Wondering Around God*, her own story, will keep anyone who has wondered about God turning the page. It won 1st place in the non-fiction memoir category and 2nd place in book cover and book design at NCPA's Annual Book Awards in 2018.

CAT MAN

DEV BERGER

I was nineteen when I met Cat Man, a thin package of mystery, who lived God-knows-where near the University of Pittsburgh.

We met at *Sam & Bernie*'s bar where I was drinking gasoline, otherwise known as ginger brandy. Ginger and brandy sound like a wonderful combination. They're not. They're something the devil concocted in his basement because together they taste like gasoline, go down like gasoline, and I foolishly drank it because my college boyfriend did.

Around ten at night, Cat Man walked into the bar and started meowing, ergo his name.

"Hi, Alex," said a number of people in the bar, many of them college students like me. Alex looked my way then meowed, and I thought he was going to lick one of his paws but he didn't. His black glasses made his goofy smile seem less so. He walked over to the pool table to watch the game. Somebody bought him a beer and he meowed again and then sat and enjoyed himself.

"Who the hell is that?" I asked Don the bartender, a rough-and-tumble social worker by day, who picked up extra cash at night serving impoverished college students and the local kooks living in the substandard housing in the area.

"Alex? He's harmless," Don said, nonplussed.

Before I could ask Don why Alex meowed, customers came in and quickly ordered beers from him.

After that evening, I saw Alex, or Cat Man which he was frequently called, either at the bar or popping up on the streets before disappearing into the darkness. His baggy pants and fraying jacket smelled like stale bread.

Remarkably, Alex was always clean-shaven and well-behaved, except once when he lunged at me after having too much to drink at the bar. My boyfriend held him back before he could have his way with me.

"Whoa there, Alex. I think you better slow down," warned my boyfriend.

Alex meowed. His eyes spun behind his glasses and his goofy smile had a sloppy madness.

Somebody corralled Alex to get him home safely in his loopy condition. Meanwhile, I wondered if there was a Mrs. Cat Man or Cat Man children at home, although I seriously doubted the possibility of either. But I wondered about Alex's mental condition, his ability to support himself, and if something had reduced this middle-aged wreckage into a creature compelled to meow.

It was in the spring when I saw Alex standing like a broken mime unable to move. He was on a street corner adjacent to Forbes Avenue and wore a clean, white shirt and his usual baggy pants. His odd, stale smell – thankfully – was in hiding. Never had I seen Alex in the daylight before. His thick, black hair hung recklessly over his forehead and he looked somber.

"Are you all right?" I asked. I waited for a meow, but it never came.

"I need cat food," he said. "For Marie. Can you get cat food?"

I'd never heard him speak so many words before and their quantity made me mute.

We were next to a store that I was fairly certain sold canned cat food.

"Wait here," I said and went inside where sure enough there were five tins of cat food for a dollar. I bought five and when I brought them to Alex, his eyes melted with a hint of tears.

"You bought cat food! Thank you."

He said it the way I imagined all the animals on Noah's Ark would have when they thanked their lucky stars to be saved from the rising waters. Alex grabbed the bag and took off like an Olympic speed walker.

Without hesitating, I followed. If Alex noticed, he gave no indication. That was fine and insulting at the same time. After a few miles of speed walking, we ended up at a dark, brown house. Alex hurried down the side of it and stopped at the back porch. He selected a tin of cat food from the bag and removed its lid. The smell of fish flew out as if it had waited years to escape. Then Alex began a series of meows that were actually eerie in how accurately they mimicked a real cat.

A few minutes later a delicate cat yowl came from the backyard. The yowls increased until finally a fetching feline appeared. Her eyes were large pools of glitter and her furry body a multi-colored shaggy rug. She moved with a grace that would put Margot Fonteyn or Rudolf Nureyev to shame. This was a ballerina come to life within a cat.

Before visiting the food, she rubbed her body so sensuously against Alex's baggy trousers that it made me yearn to be held. He spoke to her lovingly in a language that I guessed was either Serbian or Croatian, languages spoken by some of the old women in my hometown, sometimes directed harshly at me whenever I wore skimpy tops and shorts.

"Marie, Marie, Marie. Lovely Marie," Alex said in a singsong voice. She meowed and then went to the food and ate it with tiny, delicate bites, stopping occasionally to look bewitchingly at Alex.

"Is she your cat?" I asked him.

He shook his head. "Marie? My cat? Oh, no. She belongs to the world. She is too beautiful to be owned."

Again I was shocked at the mouthful of words coming from him. Did he save them up so he could use them at the end of the day with Marie?

"Is this where you live?" I asked Alex. But he wouldn't answer. All he wanted to do was watch Marie enjoying her food.

Alex sat down on the porch and after Marie finished her meal, she settled onto his lap. They meowed at one another. They were like this for a long time before I stopped watching this human Romeo with his feline Juliet. Hidden within their love story were a variety of mysteries that I could only imagine.

When I graduated from college, I still never knew where Alex lived or what happened to Marie. But I know they loved one another deeply and that she taught him the language of meows and purrs, and he taught her either Serbian or Croatian.

Their gift to me was that not all life's mysteries need to be known and that the secret lives of others are sometimes best left unexplored.

Dev Berger lives in Sacramento, CA, and was published in *Family Circle*, the *Los Angeles Times*, the *Sacramento Bee*, and *Government Technology*. She was an editor and writer for the California Federated Firefighters and worked as a writer/editor for the California Governor's Office of Criminal Justice Planning and the California State Teachers' Retirement System. She is currently working on a young adult novel.

A VERY SPECIAL DUCK

EVERETT ANSON

Hunting season was just two weeks away. Bob felt all mixed up about it. He was fourteen now. He had finally learned to handle the old 16-gauge shotgun well enough to hit clay pigeons. His father talked about the day he and Bob would go hunting together. He referred to them as "us men". Bob wondered if his father would ever consider him a man if he refused to hunt simply because he couldn't stand to see animals hurt.

On this day Bob and his father, Mr. Clark, bounced along a dirt country road with a load of firewood in the back of the pickup, a cloud of dust swirling up behind them.

Bob looked across the hills and saw a glimmer of water. Mr. Clark had seen it, too. When they rounded the next curve, he said, "Look, Bob. Those black spots on the water are ducks!"

Bob caught the excitement in his dad's voice. Bob felt it, too. "Golly, Dad! If we had our guns, we could get some ducks right now."

Even as he said it, Bob remembered how when he was about seven, he had gone along with his dad on a dove hunting trip. He had expected it to be so much fun, but the first time he saw a satin-winged dove come pummeling to the ground he turned his head away with a startled little cry.

His father had laughed. "Come on, boy," he had said, not unkindly. "If you're going to be a man, you'll have to get used to things like that."

For several nights after that, Bob cried in his pillow when he thought of the doves his father had killed that day. At that time, he couldn't even stand for his mother to kill a bug. He always asked for permission to carry it outside. Bob had grown up a lot since then. He could even kill bugs himself now. Way down inside he really did want to go hunting.

Now he heard his father saying. "I know the man who owns that property. It's Mr. Weber. I met him about a month ago. He's the one who told me where to go to get this firewood. He seems like a friendly man. I'm sure he would let us hunt there. Let's stop and ask him."

As they drove toward Mr. Weber's farm, Bob wondered what it would be like to shoot his first duck. "Golly!" Bob trembled a little. "I can hardly wait."

Mr. Clark parked the pickup and they walked up a slight hill to the house. It was an old-fashioned house with a big front porch. It had been built on a hill overlooking a fertile valley. In the distance Bob thought he could see the city. He looked through the trees and could see the sparkle of water. He recognized the lake where they had seen the ducks.

A middle-aged man, sitting in a rocking chair on the porch, stood up as they approached. His hand rested on the head of a big black Labrador dog whose tail was wagging slightly. "It's okay, Duke," he soothed, "now sit."

The dog sat down as they came up on the porch. Bob patted his head. He loved dogs. He knew instinctively this one was special.

Mr. Weber smiled and held out his hand to Bob's father. "Hello there. Did you get the firewood?"

"Yes, I did. Thank you for telling me where I could find it."

Bob thought his father would never get around to asking Mr. Weber if they could hunt. They talked about the weather, how beautiful the country was and everything except hunting. Bob knew his dad was working up to it, but he sure wished he'd get to the point. Bob could hardly wait to find out.

"You know, Mr. Weber," Mr. Clark was saying, "Bob and I saw your lake. We were wondering if you ever let anyone hunt down there. We would close the gate and be very careful. We'd pick up our empty shells and all. We'd really do our best to take care of your property."

"Hmmm," said Mr. Weber, looking down at his dog. "I'm sure you would take good care of my property, but, you see, I just don't allow hunting here."

Bob's face fell. He realized now how much he really wanted to hunt. He felt disappointed.

Mr. Weber looked at him. "Well now, hold on a bit. I don't want you to get the wrong idea about me." Mr. Weber plunged his hand into his pocket and came out with a pipe. "I'd like to explain why I don't let people hunt here, if you want to listen. Come on in while I get some tobacco."

Bob followed his father and Mr. Weber into the front room of the house. Over the fireplace hung the mounted head of a beautiful four-point buck. Hunting pictures covered the walls. Above the desk, hanging on a couple of pegs, was an old shotgun. On the desk stood a framed photograph of Mr. Weber by a flat-bottomed boat and a whole string of ducks.

"Did you shoot those ducks down by the lake?" Bob asked.

"Yes," said Mr. Weber, "but that was a long time ago. Why don't we go back on the porch and I'll tell you about it."

They went back out on the porch. Mr. Weber sat in his rocking chair. Bob curled up next to Duke and Mr. Clark sat down on a canvas-back chair to listen to what Mr. Weber had to say.

"I don't want you to think I'm keeping this property just for me and my friends to hunt. The truth is, I don't hunt anymore."

"You don't?" said Bob. "Why not?"

"Well, it's because of Duke here. Let me see. He must be about nine years old now, and I got him when he was just a pup. I got him special for hunting."

Bob looked at the dog with admiration. He wished he had a dog like that.

"The first few months Duke and I spent a good deal of time together getting used to each other. I liked to watch him. His tail didn't just wag. It seemed to go back and forth and up and down all at the same time. It was never still.

"I spent hours teaching him the things he needed to know to be a good hunting dog. He loved being out, taking orders. He learned easily." Mr. Weber leaned down and stroked the dog's head. "After Duke had been retrieving for some time, I took him to the pond down by the lake to see how he would adapt to water.

"He was retrieving sticks real well, but I happened to pitch a stick out too far one day. It lit in the reeds on the far side of the pond. When Duke went into the reeds to retrieve that stick, he sure did get excited. He came up out of there chasing something along the bank. The next thing you know, he had it. He came running up to me.

"I could tell he was carrying something in his mouth. He was carrying it carefully, a real tender mouth. I was proud of him. Then he laid it at my feet. The cutest little duck you ever saw. All brown and fuzzy.

"I looked around for any other ducks, but there were no adult ducks in the area. I figured it must have been a late hatch and the mother had taken the rest of the brood on down to the main lake where most of the ducks stayed.

"Well, at first I thought about taking the duck down to the lake, but then I thought my little girl, Nancy, would like to have that duck. I picked it up, stuck it in my coat pocket and walked on up to the house. Nancy liked the duck, but it was Duke who really took to him. When Duke would lie by the fireplace that little duck would crawl up and sit right on his head. He climbed all over Duke. They even ate out of the same dish. They really were close.

"Sometimes they'd go down to the lake together and swim. When Duke would get tired of swimming, he'd take the duck in his mouth and put him on the bank. The duck would pop to his feet and return to the water. This would go on until the duck had enough, too. Then back to the house they would come, Duke in the lead. The duck followed, not far behind with his neck stretched out, straining to keep up, as if he believed he was another dog.

"It didn't bother me any that my dog was taking up with a

wild duck because I knew as soon as the duck was old enough to fly, he would probably take off and join his wild cousins. Sure enough. The day came when the duck was gone. I figured he'd gone back to living in the wild.

"When fall came, I decided to take Duke hunting. We got down to the lake early in the morning. As the sun began to give just enough light so that we could get in some shots, I saw this lone duck come winging in off the lake. I swung up and shot. Then I gave Duke the command. He went right out to get it.

"He swam out, grasped the duck with his tender mouth and brought it in, but he didn't bring it to the blind like he'd been taught to do. He brought it up on the bank about ten feet away from me and laid it down. I had the awfullest feeling when I first saw him. I had this terrible fear that something bad was wrong.

"He sat back and watched as if he expected the duck to pop to his feet and head for the water. When nothing happened, Duke leaned forward, sniffed the duck and nudged him gently with his nose. Duke's tail stopped moving. His ears drooped and he slumped back on his haunches. He whimpered a few times. Then he laid his head back and from somewhere deep inside, he let out a howl that tore right at my guts.

"Well, I don't know if that was Duke's pet duck, but I know this. I couldn't bring myself to shoot another duck over Duke. I never went hunting again."

No one spoke for a long time after Mr. Weber had finished talking. They sat looking absently at Duke until he lifted his head and opened his mouth in a long slow yawn that sounded like a groan.

Mr. Clark laughed and the two men began talking about something else. Bob slid off the step and set off through the trees toward the lake. Duke got up and followed. It was easy to find Mr. Weber's old blind, although time and weather had nearly destroyed it. Bob sank down out of sight with a long stick as an imaginary rifle. He peered out through the reeds of the blind.

At the far end of the pond a small flock of ducks rose up

off the water and came in low toward the blind. Bob could tell by the way they came straight up off the water and by their size, they were mallards. They were not close enough to see their color. As the green heads of the drakes became distinguishable, he caught the grace and power of their wings.

Bob got to his feet and raised the stick to his shoulder sighting well ahead of the lead mallard. Just as he began to squeeze his trigger finger, a big black mass lunged through the air. It was Duke. He collided with Bob, sending him rolling back into the blind.

Bob began laughing joyously. He threw his arms around the big black dog and whispered into his ear, "Oh Duke. I wasn't really going to do it. I will never kill one of your friends! Maybe when Dad goes hunting, he will drop me off and let me spend the day with you. We'll go hunting, and I bet we can find another duck to be our own."

Everett Anson, a born storyteller and retired Electrical Engineer, graduated from Fremont Nebraska High School and served in the U.S. Navy four years. He graduated from Fresno State College and worked for the U.S. Air Force for twenty-six years including two-plus years in Germany. After retiring from the U.S. Government, he worked nine years for the California Department of Transportation. He has been married 63 years to Elva Drake. He writes short stories and has published two novels. His first book, *Bullets for Ballots*, a political thriller, brought excellent response. He decided to rewrite the story focusing on the romance. *The Third Party*, a tear-jerker, appeals to readers who like love stories. Everett's books are available at www.family1stbooks.com.

FROM 1 TO 110 AS QUICK AS A BUNNY

JULIE BEYERS

*A*s *quick as a bunny* has nothing to do with how fast a rabbit runs. In my world it had everything to do with how a simple Scouting project went from one easy-going white rabbit to 110 fluff balls that required daily care and, in some cases, air-conditioned accommodations.

It started innocently enough when my youngest son, twelve-year-old Andrew, showed an interest in his Scouting friend's rabbits. His friend was earning the *Rabbit Raising Merit Badge* and also participating in a 4-H rabbit project. As a single parent raising two teenage sons, I wanted my boys involved with established community and school programs that would provide new experiences and positive adult influence. Scouting and 4-H fit that model.

A visit to the Scouting buddy's home started us learning about rabbit care. Soon a beautiful, full grown male New Zealand White rabbit came home with my tween. We all know this rabbit – the white, twitchy nose Cadbury® bunny that sits quietly in those commercials that makes us all want to buy that amazing chocolate candy. Andrew named him 'Ty' after a country singer he admired.

It wasn't long before word got out that Andrew liked rabbits and Ty was joined by a floppy-eared lady bunny that another student at school could no longer keep. Just like that, it was twice the rabbits, twice the cages, twice the space required, but very little extra effort.

Andrew jumped in and joined 4-H to learn more about rabbits and other 4-H activities. We soon discovered rabbit shows and signed up for one. Ty and his lady friend were entered into their respective classes – New Zealand White Senior Buck and Mini Lop Senior Doe. My son was disappointed and frustrated when BOTH rabbits were disqualified. Ty was missing a toenail and the lop had a non-recognized fur color pattern, but that day Andrew decided that raising *show quality rabbits* was something he wanted to do. And so the adventure began.

Rabbit show? What the heck is that, you ask? Visualize a dog show like you've seen on TV – lots and lots of canines in kennels, pampered pups being groomed, owners scurrying with their dogs to be on time to the show ring, contemplative judges, milling crowds and a lot of crowd noise overpowered by incessant barking. Add to that ecstatic owners collecting large ribbons signifying their triumph with those winning first place, earning points towards Grand Champion status for their pooch.

Translate that vision to a rabbit show – hundreds of bunnies in carriers, small tables to groom wiggly rabbits, owners hurriedly carrying their bundle of bunny to a show table with a row of holding cages, rabbit judges, anxious onlookers and a lot of crowd noise overpowering the hundreds of nearly soundless, constantly twitching bunny noses. Enthusiastic owners collect beautiful ribbons or trophies with the first-place rabbits earning points towards Grand Champion status. Rabbit shows are organized mayhem with the softest, cutest critters and caring owners, especially at youth rabbit shows.

With show rabbits added to the collection, we needed a proper place for the rabbits to live. The only flat portion of the backyard – a place where a swing set probably entertained the children of the previous property owner – was perfect for the rows of raised cages. Field fencing was used to separate that section and to protect the rabbits from our two dogs, Lucky and Panda, who eagerly waited to catch any bunny that ventured into their part of the yard.

When we heard of some cages available at a reasonable price, we were all ears. In a pickup truck borrowed from a friend, we trekked down to the Delta to look at the cages. Unexpectedly we learned that the property was on an island, so a small ferry took us across the choppy water to the island's dock and we walked the rest of the way. When we arrived, we learned the cages came with a condition – the rabbits in the cages went with them. If we wanted the cages, we had to take the rabbits, too. There were a dozen more cages than we wanted, but the deplorable living condition of the bunnies was heart-wrenching. We took them all, including several rabbits that were very ill, because we could not in good conscience leave them there.

The mismatched multi-section cages were stacked on top of one another and secured in the back of the pickup after a harrowing, overloaded ferry ride. With some of the cages hanging over the tailgate, we didn't have safe spaces for each rabbit. We weren't planning on getting rabbits and hadn't brought carriers. That meant that some rabbits had to be doubled up – something that is never a good idea. We tried to ignore odd looks and obvious laughter from other drivers as we drove the 50+ miles home with the hodgepodge of cages and rabbits, some that spent the entire trip actively engaged in activities bunnies are famous for. Except for the busy bunnies, it was an uneventful trip home.

The newly purchased cages and the odd assortment of rabbits had to go somewhere. A quick sketch, several phone calls, and amazing support from Contractor Steve led to construction, at the top of our steep hillside property, of several strong but basic 'pole barns'. The barns consisted of three round posts on the long sides, each reaching ten-feet above the ground, supporting crossbeams and basic rafters, all covered by a large, bright blue tarp held in place by the weight of dirt-filled tube socks dangling from every other grommet on the sides of each tarp. The 'barns' looked ridiculous, but were practical and amazingly effective at protecting the rabbits from the sun, wind and rain.

The cages were suspended from the crossbeams by chains, allowing the rabbit poop to accumulate under the cages. Funny thing about free-falling rabbit poop. When left alone and not mixed with sawdust, it doesn't smell or attract many flies, an important consideration since the horses boarded next door contributed to the neighborhood fly population. High in nitrogen from a rabbit's typical diet of pellets and grass hay, rabbit poop can be scooped from under the cages directly into the garden. Our neighbors were happy to get a call when the poop got too deep. We called, they came and all the bunny poop went to good homes. It was rewarding to know we were contributing to the good health of neighboring vegetable gardens and landscaping.

Sadly, the sick rabbits we brought home from the Delta continued to get sicker and we had no choice but to put them down. Our neighbor, Rick, helped dispatch them to bunny heaven and we buried them under a canopy of scrub oaks and digger pines. Imagine our shock when two days later, we discovered tufts of rabbit fur scattered across our hillside. Apparently we didn't bury them deep enough and some of our local coyotes dug them up for a late-night dinner. A thoughtful discussion about the food chain and the circle of life ensued.

Andrew obtained a group of pedigreed New Zealand Whites of various bloodlines with rabbits bought at shows or from visits to nearby rabbit ranches, and from one fortuitous trip to a small animal auction located some 25 miles away. He developed a successful line of quality show rabbits, including one young rabbit that won a national competition.

The small animal auction was key and a total fluke. The remaining rabbits from the Delta needed to go somewhere else to create cage space for future New Zealands, so a trek to the small animal auction was needed. I made the trip with my friend, Catherine, who was visiting while my sons spent the weekend at their dad's house. We took four rabbits of unknown descent to sell at the auction. By an awesome stroke of pure luck, we were at the auction *on the one day that year* when a nationally recognized breeder was culling his herd of White and Red New Zealands. I bid high enough to win the bid for the first white rabbit. By the rules of the auction, I was then able to buy the remaining six white rabbits for the same price. A handshake agreement allowed Andrew to contact the breeder after the auction to obtain pedigrees for each of the rabbits. These rabbits became his foundation stock.

Getting home from the auction with more rabbits than we went to the auction with was an adventure itself. While I protected the rabbits from other auction attendees wanting to take them home for dinner, Catherine scrounged up some boxes to transport rabbits. Four rabbits went in the carrier, which left three rabbits for the cardboard boxes. Catherine, allergic to rabbit fur, spent the entire ride home in the back of the minivan surrounded by bunnies attempting to escape the boxes, which did not close. After we got the rabbits settled into cages at home, we made a mad dash to the pharmacy for allergy medication. Poor Catherine spent the evening doped up on medication and scratching like crazy. Only a good friend would do such a selfless act. We laughed about it later...much later.

At some point in our rabbit adventure, Andrew fell in love with one of the smallest types of rabbits called the Ruby-Eyed White Netherland Dwarf – small white bundles with short ears and piercing red eyes. Where a New Zealand rabbit can weigh up to 12 pounds, Netherland Dwarfs have a top weight of 2.5 pounds. The contrast between the breeds was amazing and Andrew was the only competitor we knew of who bred and showed both breeds.

To obtain some quality Netherland Dwarfs, we drove all the way to Los Angeles to meet a well-known breeder of Netherlands. We planned to only acquire three or four bunnies so we took a single four-slot carrier. Two days later we returned home with an additional carrier and a total of seven rabbits, six white and one black with striking white markings.

The smaller rabbits were less hardy and more susceptible to temperature changes than the New Zealands that live outdoors. Therefore, different accommodations were needed. The petite bunnies lived in my bedroom in our largest carriers until proper cages could be procured. Eventually we obtained a bank of stacking cages with six cages that took over the space next to the kitchen table in the breakfast nook. The kitchen table held one cage and miscellaneous supplies. The seven rabbits in the house joined our growing herd. Good thing we had a dining room table so there was a place to sit and eat that wasn't in front of the TV or on the living room couch.

As the herd grew and Andrew continued to improve his breeding stock, we enhanced the pole barns and backyard cage area with electricity for lights and for fans during the hot summer months. Andrew braved summer heat and winter cold in his bedroom as his screen-free window remained open year-round so two 100-foot extension cords could supply power from a wall outlet to the pole barns and backyard cage area. It was far from ideal, but Andrew's commitment to his rabbits shone brightly every day.

Connections with other rabbit enthusiasts were made through 4-H, rabbit shows and local contacts. Each year several female New Zealands, known as does, were bred to Andrew's award-winning bucks so that litters of rabbits were ready in time for a local fair. Annually, other 4-H members bought rabbits from Andrew to show at the fair or at local rabbit shows. Rabbits originally bred at his rabbitry consistently won top honors at local fairs. His breeding program also generated additional rabbits when litters of seven or eight babies were born to each of several does. The numbers added up quickly. One bunny in a cage suddenly became as many as nine bunnies in a cage 30 to 32 days after a doe hung out with a buck for mere moments. Here is where the original meaning of "as quick as a bunny" is really relevant.

However, it was one of those community connections that swelled our usually manageable rabbitry to a ridiculous level...and they weren't even our rabbits. A friend of a friend, let's call him Bunny Bob, had problems with his rabbitry. His twelve rabbits took up residence in space outside of our fenced rabbit area while Bunny Bob rebuilt his barn. Bob provided the cages and food, coming by several times a week to check the bunnies.

Andrew had plenty to do with our 30+ rabbits, so I took

on the daily care of Bob's bunnies. I made sure they had food and water, and frozen water bottles on really hot days. Our entire garage freezer was dedicated to frozen bottles of water to put into rabbit cages on those days when an oscillating fan, and misting the rabbits, didn't seem to be enough. One day I came home from work to find all twelve of Bob's rabbits out of their cages. A special needs boy in the neighborhood had released all of Bob's bunnies. I caught ten of the rabbits, recovered the body of one rabbit killed in a neighbor's yard by their dog, and searched fruitlessly for the twelfth rabbit. That night I called Bunny Bob to explain the situation and plan for the future of his rabbits. The missing rabbit was returned by neighbors a week later after news of the incident spread. So let me tell you all you need to know about rabbit husbandry and quick bunnies. A month later, Bob's eleven remaining bunnies became 32 when all seven of his does gave birth.

With a majority of Andrew's does having litters in preparation for fair time, we now had 110 rabbits to care for. Rabbit care took hours each day, making sure each rabbit had clean water, food, a frozen water bottle, misting and working fans. On hot days, all the nesting boxes were moved each morning to the kitchen table in our air-conditioned house and returned to their moms each evening for their nighttime feeding. This schedule kept the babies from overheating during the day and allowed the does to nurse twice a day as they usually did. We kept up that schedule for several weeks, then rejoiced when Bob took his 32 bunnies home to their refurbished barn.

This amazing journey from a single bunny to breeding a national award-winning rabbit and dominating the local fair scene spanned almost five years. With college looming, Andrew's rabbits found new placements including some going to a New Zealand breeder in Canada. The cages and supplies were sold, and the blue tarps removed leaving the pole barns for another adventure.

You would be astounded at the number of times Andrew,

a talented teenage magician, pulled a white rabbit out of a hat. But that's a story for another time.

In her work life, Julie did accounting, internal auditing, and wrote contracts, white papers, board memos and grant applications. Her editing skills were utilized by all of her employers. She contributed an article to the May 2016 issue of *The Nugget Magazine*, a trade publication of the Sacramento District Dental Society, as part of her work to improve the oral health of young children and their families. During her years living in Auburn, California, she led a writers group, *The Placer Word Miners*, for five years, creating writing prompts, meeting exercises and sponsoring community open mic events.

Now retired and living in Northern California, Julie continues to dabble in poetry and short creative pieces while utilizing her strengths in reviewing, editing, and grant writing to help others. She is available to authors to consult on any length project and to non-profits to develop grant application content and strategies.

Contact Julie through her website, www.juliebeyers.com

IN THE MIDDLE

BARBARA YOUNG

"Yay, it's another sunny day!" I take a peek. Not enough to wake up, but just enough to confirm that I am warm, with my fluffy dolly and red blanky in my cozy bed. I listen for my mommy and daddy's voices. I'm excited because I hear them and I know that they will come see me soon.

My mommy's voice gets louder as she comes down the stairs, calling my name and asking "What's our Sunny Boy doing? Is he a good boy? I think he's a good boy and he's been sleeping."

Ummmm. It feels sooooo gooooood to stretch from my nose to my toes as she rubs down my back. I look up at her from the corner of my eye. She thinks I'm so cute and I get more cuddles and nuzzles. Here comes Daddy too. He rubs my ears, pats my belly and tells me that I am a good boy. Wow, this is my favorite thing, to be in the middle, where I feel cherished and adored.

I bask and recall a fading memory of my other life when I was lost and roaming the rainy streets. Then it was cold and lonely, but it was a sunny day when I met my guardian dog-angel. I had never seen any other dog that looked like me, white with black spots, so I knew it must be true that he was mine. He told me we were Dalmatians. He said that when he became an angel, his first job was to find another dog for his mommy and daddy to cherish and adore, as soon as they were ready. Lucky for me, they were almost ready. He knew I was a good dog who needed a home and people to cherish and adore me.

My guardian dog-angel spoke to me in my dreams and guided me to the care of some nice people. I had a cough and they helped me get better. But they were not *my* people. They took me to a home where there were dogs that looked like me everywhere! It was fun to frolic and roll around with other Dalmatians. This was a really special home where spots were respected. There were beds and blankets with spots, spotted bowls, and even toys with spots.

One day, one *sunny* day, I dashed through the doggie door from the backyard just like I always did. But this time when I looked up, I met the eyes of two new people. Without hesitation, I ran to them and they were already on the floor with waiting laps. These were *my* people; I knew it in my heart! We played, I showed them how cute I could be, and we walked around the yard. Then they opened the door to a car.

Were we going for a ride in their car? I jumped inside and lay still on the seat, hardly able to believe this was happening. They sat at my side, each keeping a hand on me while we rode to where I had dreamed, my new home. These were *my* people and I was in the middle!

I hear morsels clinking in my bowl. That is a good reason to get out of bed because my tummy really wants them. I carry my fluffy dolly in my mouth and set it beside my bowl where it waits for me. My tail wags a lot when I eat. Sometimes it even goes in circles. The faster it twirls, the faster I eat. My mommy and daddy call it my "happy meter."

After my tummy is full, I go find Mommy and Daddy sitting on the couch. I have three dollies that are all shaped like bones. I have a fluffy dolly, a red dolly, and my very special car dolly I play with when I go for a ride in the car. They are all good dollies, and I am good to my dollies because I never tear them apart. I nibble on my red dolly and make it squeak, then I wiggle and roll around with my dolly. Mommy sits on the floor so I can get in her lap. She rubs all the tension from my muscles. Daddy leans down, touches the tip of my nose, pats me and then joins us on the floor. Ah, I'm in the middle.

Daddy finishes his coffee and says, "Sunny Boy, Let's go feed the horses." I spring up from Mommy's lap, grab my red dolly, and wait with excitement by the door. As Daddy and I go down the driveway, I hold my happy meter high. It sways side to side and I lift my step as I prance my way to the barn.

We have ten horses. Once I touched noses with a horse and its nose was a lot bigger than mine.

Daddy calls me Snoop because I help by snooping around so Daddy doesn't have to feed the horses alone.

We sprinkle corn on the ground for Mr. Doodle, the rooster, and the doves come to eat. Mr. and Mrs. Mallard fly in for breakfast along with sparrows and robins.

I have a fun yard. It is big and I am never alone. There are squirrels up in the trees, along with the birds. There is also a big hawk who visits. He mostly stays up high and watches over me.

I have my own ducks and geese. Daddy and I feed them every morning. We open the door and they have a committee meeting right outside their pen. They will stay busy waddling around the yard rooting for bugs all day. But their favorite thing to do is find my bowl of water or a sprinkler to play in.

Daddy and I walk around and look at things in the yard. I see the wild turkeys walking across the bridge to my yard. They are friendly and don't mind us passing by. Turkeys do funny things like follow each other around in circles and stand on the picnic table. They are big birds, but one time, they suddenly got even bigger, right in front of me! They puffed up to show off, and spread out their fancy tail feathers.

Down by the creek there are clues that many animals have visited my ranch. At night while I am sleeping inside my house, they walk around my yard and leave a trail of messages. In the morning I get to know them by their smell, and follow their tracks to figure out what they were doing in my yard. I leave messages for them too, via "pee mail".

After the morning chores, I go to my favorite spot to lie in the sun, a patch of grass in the cove between the garden, the hedge and the rose bushes. It's out of the wind and the usual squirrel scamper trails. Lucy, the big dog next door, cannot see me there so she doesn't bark. I position myself to keep a watchful eye on the driveway gate, the front door and the garage door. My red dolly lies with me and sometimes Mr. Doodle does too.

I awake to see Mommy and Daddy swinging on the front porch swing so I run over to see if they will let me ride. They pet me and my ears splay out sideways then slightly crinkle. Mommy and Daddy know what my goofy ears are asking. Daddy scoops me up onto the swing. They both pet me and tell me I'm a "good Sunny Boy." I sit up straight and proud, with their cheeks to mine, until the motion makes me sleepy. I rest my muzzle on Mommy's lap. This time she gets the *thinkin'* end and Daddy gets the *stinkin'* end. I drift into sleep, comfy and in the middle.

After my nap I jump down from the swing and run to the front door. I like to be the first one *at* the door, so I can be the first one *in* the door. Sometimes Mommy and Daddy ask me to "sit" and "stay" because *they* want to be first. I don't always get "the stay" part perfect, but I still get to go inside, even though they get to be first.

Daddy asks me, "Where's your red dolly?"

I sniff around and look everywhere. It's not in my bed. My white dolly is by my bowl, but I need my red dolly. It's not by the couch or anywhere on the floor.

"It must be outside. Go back out and get your dolly."

He opens the door and I run around the yard. I find my dolly where we were lying in the sun. I pick it up in my mouth and run fast to get inside and jump in my bed before Daddy can close the door.

After I doze with my dolly, I see Mommy and Daddy on the couch talking and laughing. I sit by their feet and they pet me. Somehow, they get distracted and stop. They are still talking but not about my dolly or dinner, going for a walk or a ride in the car. I suckle my dolly for comfort. Since I haven't heard them say anything about me for a while, I better do something cute to get their attention. I suddenly point my nose straight up in the air toward them to say, "Hey, I'm so cute...don't forget about me!" This gets their attention. They laugh and their conversation is about me again.

I twist around and put my head on Daddy's lap. First a hand or two and then all four of Mommy's and Daddy's hands are petting me. I leverage a better position by standing up. My happy meter is going strong. Mommy and Daddy are laughing and say I'm a good boy. I want to be closer to them, so I raise my front paws up and plop them onto their laps. They each get a paw and I scoot my belly up there too. I feel my goofy ears coming on, but I don't hear "No."

By standing on my back tippy toes, my happy meter gives me momentum to quickly lift my third paw up and then the last one. This is nice. I lie motionless.

They ask, "*Whaaaat are yoooou doing?*" The tip of my tail quivers and I look up at Daddy from the corner of my eye and then at Mommy. They hug me, pet me, and laugh. This feels good. I know in my heart that I'm meant to be a lap dog! These are *my* people. It only took four years to lap train them, and I'm in the middle.

Barbara Young is Mommy to the Dalmatian, Sunny, in this story. They live with Sunny's Daddy, Steve, on a ranch in Northern California. Barbara's recently published book, *The Heart that Rocks Health Care,* is available on Amazon. She also writes poetry and is currently working on a Sunny Boy children's book series. Learn more at www.byoungbooks.com.

MY NAME IS JOHN PAUL

DENISE LEE BRANCO

I was born atop hay, tucked beneath stair-stepped bales that elevated into the sky. The private place where my birth mom brought me and my siblings into the world felt cozy and safe. I thought it would be my forever home, where I would see my birth mom's face and snuggle next to her and my siblings as I matured. Instead, the body warmth which embraced me at birth evaporated that very next morning and I was all alone.

The farmer's wife saw me as she approached the haystack for her morning chores. I was a tiny black and white fur ball, and she couldn't figure out what she was seeing until she drew closer. My eyes were not yet open to the world, but I knew in my heart that the farmer's wife was my guardian angel. God created me and sent me into this world through my feline mama, but this human mama was destined to be my true mother for life.

My first year was both exciting and tough. Mama didn't get much sleep for a few weeks. She warmed newborn kitten formula and fed it to me every three hours with an eye dropper bottle. A cardboard box lined and loosely covered with kitchen towels became my humble abode. Mama wouldn't leave me home alone, so I got to go with her everywhere. I loved traveling with her in my comfy cardboard home.

Though I could not see, I heard sweet, tender voices all around me. Wherever I went, people wanted to pet me. Everyone liked watching Mama feed me with the eye dropper bottle. I kept hearing them say, "Aww, he's so cute!" and "He's adorable!" Mama loved sharing my story and seeing others adore me as much as she did. It brought her immense joy being the mom God chose for me.

Though my human mama tried her best to provide me with proper nutrition every few hours, I was deprived of those vital early nutrients from my feline mama. That deficiency landed me at the doctor's office and emergency room on more than one occasion. There was an interesting vibe in waiting rooms when my name was called. It was like people were scanning the area for a celebrity who had just made his entrance. Mama explained to onlookers that my name was John Paul and I had been named in honor of Pope John Paul who had passed away the day I was born. Pope John Paul was admired by Catholics around the world, and for Mama to name me that made me feel very important and special.

Despite health setbacks my first year, I grew up to be a fine young man. Mama said I was a quick study when it came to potty training. I ate real kitten food as soon as I felt up to it. I even discovered a love for country western music. I'd jump up on the armrest of our couch and wait there until Mama would see me. That was my cue to get her to come turn on our vintage stereo console. She got a kick out of watching the music serenade me to sleep.

I've tried to be a great son for Mama. I like keeping her lap warm when we're sitting in her favorite easy chair and comforting her as she strokes my fur from head to tail. At night when she rests her head on her pillow, I outstretch my paw to the side of her neck, set my lips on hers, and give her a quick goodnight kiss. I do my best every day to show her how much I love her.

Life, however, became much more demanding after my namesake was declared a saint. Pope John Paul entered sainthood in April of 2014 and living up to his greatness has been stressful on me.

I've always lived indoors, but once I tore through our screen door and ended up outside. I thought I had seen my late big sister, Sassy, out by the birch tree. Sassy was adopted by my Mama four years before me and she was motherly just like Mama. I'll never forget how Sassy let me snuggle with her for

hours and hours when I was a baby. We were very close.
Before Sassy left, my instincts told me that Sassy wasn't
feeling well. She had aged and grown ill, but I never imagined
that she'd leave our home and not return. She'd been gone for
five days and I missed her terribly. I could have sworn that I
saw her by the birch tree that late spring day.

When I realized that Sassy wasn't in our backyard, I
became frightened. Hearing sounds high in the sky and
stepping on bark-covered ground were foreign to me. I
panicked and squeezed under the fence. I could hear my canine
stepsister barking in the distance. She was in our house and
trying her best to help. I kept listening to her and crawled
alongside my house all the way to the front porch. I was very
scared, but I stayed there. That's where I hoped someone
would find me.

Both of my parents were searching for me. Papa found me
first. He picked me up and brought me inside. Oh, how nice it
was to see my canine stepsister and be in the comforts of home
again! Mama combed the neighborhood for quite a while. She
asked anyone she came across in her search to keep watch for
me. When Papa saw Mama at the end of our block facing
home, he waved at her to come back.

Mama feared the worst had happened and she didn't want
to give up looking for me, but Papa's persistent wave meant
that she needed to get home. When Mama arrived back home
and saw me, water started pouring from her eyes. I hadn't seen
her eyes do that before, but I sensed she felt relieved that her
prayers were answered.

Three years later I became frustrated for some unknown
reason and lashed out at my mama. I bit her arm much too
deeply. The area got infected and not only did she need medical
treatment, but the urgent care doctor reported my actions to
the animal police. They came to my home and filled out
paperwork about my actions. The stern, khaki-uniformed lady
sentenced me to one week on house arrest. She found me and
Mama completely healthy by week's end and our case was
closed.

I'm embarrassed to say that I lashed out at Mama a few weeks after that incident. I don't know what came over me, but we ended up in the same scenario. The animal officer came to my home again and she looked at me that time with added disappointment. My second case was also closed without issue.

I've done my best to redeem myself and gain Mama's trust back since my temper tantrums. My behavior has improved tremendously, so much so that she gives me an extra treat of Friskies Party Mix right before bedtime. It's fantastic to end the night on a happy note!

I will always be thankful to Mama for helping me through life and loving me in the good times and bad. Our heart connection is genuine. I don't need to wonder what life would have been like if I had grown up with my birth mother because I've had a wonderful life! I thank God for bringing me into this world and placing me in the hands of this different type of mom. I know He planned it all from the day that she cradled me in her caring hands at the haystack. I have no doubt that Mama will continue to be there for me, looking into my eyes with adoration and devotion, until the moment God calls me home.

Denise Lee Branco is an award-winning author and inspirational speaker, who continues to believe, dream, and overcome so those who meet her recognize the possibilities within them. Denise's first book, *Horse at the Corner Post: Our Divine Journey*, won a silver medal in the Living Now Book Awards.

Denise is a member of the Cat Writers Association, California Writers Club-Sacramento, Christian Indie Publishing Association, Independent Book Publishers Association, Inspire Christian Writers, and Northern California Publishers and Authors (NCPA). She has been a contributor to multiple anthologies. Denise is currently working on her next book(s). She lives in Northern California, and besides writing faith-filled inspirational stories, she loves spending time with and spoiling her three rescues. It is her honor to share the story of her parents' beloved fur child, John Paul, in this anthology. Follow Denise on Twitter @DeniseLeeBranco and visit www.DeniseInspiresYou.com to learn more.

SUNDAY, SUNDAY

A.K. BUCKROTH

"Hon, will you go for a walk with me please?" asked the newlywed wife. "I need some exercise, but I'd like you to go to the market with me as well. We need milk, and you'll have to carry that home."

"Ohoho, you don't wanna go alone because of that guy that beeped at you the other day," replied the husband with a grin. "Sure, I'll go with you, but why do I have to carry the milk home? What else are you going to get?"

"A gallon of milk is too heavy for me to carry. The other things I want to get are a loaf of sourdough bread, large brown eggs, a bag of baby carrots, a stalk of celery and a white onion for chicken soup, along with a jar of chicken bouillon cubes, and some much-needed bird seed."

"What about the chicken?"

"I have that. It's defrosting in the kitchen sink."

"Why don't we just drive over there?" he asked.

"Nope. Walk first. It's a total of one mile around the block. On the way home, we can stop at the store."

"Yah, but I know you," husband said with a cheeky grin and a twinkle in his eye. "You'll end up getting 15 bags of stuff! We should probably take the wagon."

"No. I'll only buy those things I mentioned. Promise."

"Okay then. Before we go, let me feed Aksamio and Tweety first. It's close to their dinnertime anyway and I'll give them the rest of this bird food."

Agreeing, the wife accompanied her husband from their galley kitchen, down the wide, carpeted hall to their bright, naturally lit two-car garage. The cockatiels, Aksamio and Tweety, were loudly heard as the couple approached the heavy wooden door leading into the garage. The cockatiels always knew when the humans were coming, together or separately, talking their excited chirp-talk.

"Tweet, tweet," squeaked Tweety delicately, as she looked up at them. She was cleaning her yellow and white wing feathers, side-to-side, awaiting her feeding.

"MWEEP, MWEEP," hollered Aksamio loudly as usual. Puffing out his yellow, green and grey feathered chest, he stepped from one bar perch to another like he was aggravated. *You humans aren't moving fast enough* could've been his haughty reply. The wife found this amazing to watch as Aksamio opened his beak wide as if to speak, showing his skinny pink tongue.

"Gosh, hon, it bothers me that Aksamio is so loud. He makes me think he's angry. He's like this all the time. I don't think he likes me. He's better with you, being a man. A man-to-man cock, cock, cockatiel." She burst out laughing at her own joke.

Her husband smiled widely, a bit of a blush on his cheeks as he opened the wheeled four-foot-high, two-foot-wide bird cage and gave the birds fresh water from the garage sink and bird seed from the homemade hardwood pantry.

"Tweety likes me," declared the wife. "She'll climb on my finger when I put it in front of her belly. You wanna see?"

"No, not now if you wanna go for that walk. Let's go."

Leaving the garage the way they entered, Tweety softly squeaked as if saying '*See ya later*' with a mouthful of food. Aksamio? Well, he didn't give a crap, literally. Such differing personalities these two had, even though they had been together since they were eggs.

Merrily walking down the street on this warm Sunday in April, the wife heard a familiar "tweet tweet." Assuming it came from a nearby apartment complex, she whistled in kind. The "tweet tweet, tweet tweet" weakly continued, but she couldn't see the bird.

"Do you hear that?" she asked her husband. "It sounds like another cockatiel. Maybe over there," she pointed, continuing to whistle. It responded! "Oh my gosh! I hope it's okay."

"It's fine. I'm sure. It's probably hungry like our birds."

Continuing to the grocers and after getting everything on the list, the wife included some miniature chocolate donuts. The husband liked those. With a one-handled bag for her, and the gallon of milk for him to carry, they were able to continue their walk home, holding hands.

Curious, they decided to walk on the opposite side of the street, wondering about the bird they heard. Slowly approaching the same area, the tweeting picked up, stronger, louder. "Hon, that bird is calling us. I know it!" the wife declared.

"How do you know that? How *would* you know that?" sarcasm filled the husband's voice.

"I just do," she stated with confidence. "Wait. Give me a minute. Stand still while I whistle and you listen for its response. It will respond." Doing that, the bird, in fact, did respond.

"It's close," he said. "Oh my God, look! There it is! In the parking lot. On the ground. That hard top is hot! I gotta go get it, save it."

"Oh my, she's beautiful! Okay, be careful climbing over that parking lot barrier chain. Don't move quickly but hurry up! You don't want to frighten her. Put the milk down." She rested the groceries on the sidewalk. "Looks like she may have gotten out of her cage and tried to fly away."

Gently cupping her in both hands, the husband proudly showed his wife, smoothing the bird's wing feathers, cooing to her at the same time.

With concern, the wife asked, "Is there is any blood on her? Any broken feathers or bones? How are her talons?"

This white-on-white cockatiel didn't fight her captor, didn't peck, bite or claw the husband's hands. The wife was momentarily stunned at the gentleness they expressed to each other.

"Nope, she looks fine to me so far. I'll get a better look when we get home." Walking steadily and quickly, holding the bird close to his heart, the husband made long strides. "I'll meet you at the house. Grab the grub."

"Yep, yep," she hollered to his fast-moving back. "I can't wait to see her, make sure she's okay. And don't put her in the cage with Tweety and Aksamio."

"Why not?" He turned to ask her. "Nevermind. I'll put her in the little cage after I get it down from the rafters. She'll have to stay in the garage sink for a few minutes. That'll cool off her hot little feet, poor thing."

Off he went.

Yes, the wife ended up carrying the gallon of milk home with the bag of groceries. This took her longer than she anticipated, the weight of her purchases a bit cumbersome.

Finally back at home and hurriedly placing the groceries inside the entryway, she could hear the birds screaming! All of them! Standing in the garage doorway, her husband was turning around and around, comically, with a butterfly net in one hand trying to coax the white cockatiel off the garage door cables. The bird cried loudly causing the others to participate. It haphazardly flew from one cable to the other, atop storage boxes, down to the floor, then up to a cable again.

"Sh…Sh…Sh…" the wife started. "Hon. HON! Stop! Stay still. You're making her and the others nervous. Put your hands down, gently lay down that silly net, and stand still. Leave her be."

"But…but…but…" the husband stammered.

She coaxed him out of the garage with her, and only then did Tweety and Aksamio calm their tempos.

Thirty minutes later, silence ensued. The wife slowly, gently, opened the garage door once again. Captivated at seeing this beautiful bird fly around and around the garage, she stood still, in awe of her wondrous wing span. Watching, the wife waited a few minutes before the bird flew to where the other two were housed and sat atop their large metallic cage.

"So, little bird," the wife spoke to the newcomer. "Are you done showing off? How about if I put you in that smaller cage over there?"

Holding out her arm in confidence, she slowly neared the white bird, placing a finger near her belly. She hopped up onto the wife's finger! Delighted, the wife slowly walked, staring eye-to-eye with the creature, placing her in the smaller nearby cage. Good thing it was handy! As she readied the food and water, *Whitey* began nibbling seeds and wetting her beak.

"Wow. You did it," remarked the husband, rather shocked. "Good job."

Watching this beautiful white cockatiel was astounding. Her temperament became calm and accepting...likeable. She had been taken care of. After purposely separating her from Tweety and Aksamio, she was able to stay nearby them in their suite to get acquainted.

"Gosh, she's like a dream come true, you know that?" commented the wife. "Seeing as you saw her first, what would you like to name her?"

"Sunday. Her name will be Sunday because we found her on Sunday."

"Oh, that's perfect. I like it."

"And by the way," the husband asked, "how did you know she's a she?"

"I just did. Magic," she replied with a twinkle in her eye.

But really? Male cockatiels have orange cheeks. Aksamio had round orange cheeks whereas Tweety — and now Sunday — did not.

Mystery solved.

A Sacramento County, California resident since 2004, A. K. Buckroth's yearning to write came to fruition in 2010. Her first book, *My Diabetic Soul – An Autobiography,* granted her six awards: three in California, two in Massachusetts, and one from Indiana. This led her to become a Global Diabetes Advocate where she continues to articulate her message of diabetes awareness while promoting this book.

Enlightenment encouraged her to proceed. There followed a set of three self-published books: *Me & My Money...*, *Me & My Money Too...*, and lastly *Kisses for Cash...*, which won third place in the NCPA 2017 Book Awards Young Adult Category. Each will witness updated versions expected to be published in 2019 with a historical fiction, a new genre for AK. A biography is also in her mind's eye in the sky as the sky has no limits.

SO CLOSE AND YET SO FAR

NORMA JEAN THORNTON

We have three cats. Loving, lovable Dobby, the oldest at 7 years, is a brownish-gray striped short-haired male tabby, 6-year-old Windy, a long-haired Main-Coon-Cat look-alike beauty, who has her own diary, and Severus, the under-a-year-old baby, with luscious shiny, thick-long-black-fur, and an equally long, fluffy, gorgeous tail – way too pretty to be a male.

This story is about Severus.

* * *

It was still light out, but late on a chilly Sunday afternoon the first week of November, and as usual, after being outside off and on all day, Dobby came in from the backyard first, with Windy following close behind ... but where was Severus?

He was normally hot on Windy's tail, fighting to be second, but instead, always making it a tight third since he was so easily distracted by everything, even just a spot on the ground, that looked interesting.

Severus, not playing follow-the-leader though, in case he might miss out on something those other two were going to get into, was unusual in itself, but even more so when I went out back to call for him and he didn't come.

Nor did he show his presence while just staying out of reach, as he always did when he wasn't ready to stop lurking in the tall grass or playing in the great outdoors, to relinquish all of his outside fun and come in the house.

Why should he? All of his favorite play things were out there ... graceful butterflies flitting around, noisy blue jays and magpies that sometimes dive-bombed him ... bright-colored dragonflies and buzzing bees to jump high after and often catch, at times to his dismay ... crawling bugs and creepy-crawly-worms to push around with his nose, rather than pick them up in his mouth, because they're squishy and squiggle around, frequently even trying to crawl up his nose and in his eyes ... the bright warm sun that he loves to bask in, and the two large oak trees he enthusiastically climbs way to the top of, with lots of little branches along the way to help him back down, as he generally still comes down the same way he goes up ~ all twenty claws dug tightly into the tree bark, with head pointing to the sky and long, fluffy tail hesitantly flipping back and forth as he slowly descends, tail first.

Two cats inside, one still out. Severus was flat nowhere to be seen.

For almost forty-eight hours!

* * *

Two grandkids who were visiting, thoroughly scoured the neighborhood for Severus that evening, while I called, whistled (yes, whistled; all of our cats come to my special whistle, to the tune of *"Shave and a Haircut 6 Bits!"*), and meowed for him into the chilly wee hours of the following morn to no avail.

Bright and early that freezing-cold Monday morning, I was outside calling for him again, and fretting because there was frost on the grass and the water in the birdbath was partially frozen over.

Off and on all that day, I was out back meowing, calling and whistling more, but no Severus.

Even though the cats rarely went into the front yard, a couple of times I still wandered out front, half-heartedly making noises for Severus, but my fear was that he'd gone over the back fence and suffered the same fate our last little black kitty had – the three dogs running loose in their owner's one-and-a-half-acre yard.

I made a phone call, but the neighbors weren't home, and

I couldn't even go over into their yard to look for the cat, because of those dogs.

I moped around the second day, voting-day-Tuesday, putting off going to vote until after dark, just in case that fluffy, shiny, long-haired black beauty came home, but I got a phone call at 4:30 PM that something needed to be picked up in less than a half-hour. I got dressed and headed out the door.

The grinding, squeaky noises from our heavy black-wrought-iron gate as it creaked across my concrete driveway while sliding open couldn't mask a pathetic meow coming from across the street.

I stopped pushing the gate, and listened ...

There it was ... a soft *"meow"*.

I meowed back.

An indignant *"%$$%$MEOW!!!#@##$"* response.

I called "Severus!"

Suddenly multiple meows, each one more urgent: *Meow!MEow!!MEOw!!!MEOW!!!!*

Exactly where was the meowing coming from? It sounded like all over. First one yard, then the other, of the two homes facing back-to-back across the street from ours.

It was impossible to see anything through those tiny slits, which were between the pieces of wood that formed the side-fence of the house to the left, where the initial sounds were. But now, the meowing that had appeared to be coming from the back of that house with the wooden fence, instead was coming from the house on the right that had a chain-length side-fence surrounding it.

I walked further towards the yard of the house on the right that I could see in. Suddenly, the meowing came from above!

My eyes searched for a little black bundle possibly hidden in one of those nine trees, including palm and tall cedars, but no oak, that stood between the two backyards along the neighbors' back fence line.

Fortunately, Severus moved at just the right time in that tiny little nook he had found, way up high in the super-tall, barren, huge tree with smooth bark; so smooth, that he couldn't get a grip on it, or stick a claw into, to try to climb down.

Climb down from his perch in a tree where he could be seen that whole time … from our bedroom window, and the computer I'm typing this on … had I just known …

The neighbor with the wooden fence had two dogs. Without a doubt, the little guy had somehow gotten into their yard, and running scared, moved quickly up that tree to escape the dogs, and true to his nature, went almost all the way to the top.

The other neighbors speak no English, and as I attempted to remember what little Spanish I could, she understood what I needed, so allowed me in her backyard, and thankfully sent her kids to get their commercial ladder.

When he saw me, Severus tried to climb down, but couldn't make it beyond two partial kitty-steps.

He's rarely been able to come face-first down a tree, especially one that doesn't have a bunch of leaves and tiny branches that he can support himself with, and this one had nothing. It's a wonder he even managed to climb it at all, let alone as high as he did. He must have been petrified!

Normally, he scoots down backwards, but he was having none of that at this point. He was close to twenty-feet up that almost thirty-foot tall tree.

Even though I'm terrified of heights, especially ladders, I cautiously climbed the neighbor's tall ladder, for what good it did, while clinging on for dear life, to try to coax that cat closer to me, but he was having no part of that, either. Severus was meowing constantly by now, so I called in some support – the granddaughters' 6-foot-tall boyfriend, who fortunately lived right around the corner.

Almost an hour after Severus was found, he was finally saved.

The boyfriend climbed the ladder to the very top and stretched his arm high, barely grabbed Severus by the tip of his long gorgeous bushy tail and pulled the terrified cat towards him.

That little snot's lucky he had such long thick fur, and didn't get a frostbitten nose and tootsies, on all four little footsies, since it was below freezing the two nights that he apparently was stuck up in that tree ... within my sight ... so close, and yet so far!

Her baby sister called her Nonie, her great-granddaughter calls her GumGum.

Norma Jean Thornton, AKA Noniedoodles & Granny-GumGum, is a multiple County and State Fair award-winning baker, candy-maker and art-doodler, plus an award-winning writing granny from Rio Linda, California, who dabbles with her writings at the computer, and attempts to create her doodle-art, with unwanted help from her feisty cats.

lulu.com/spotlight/nonie
lulu.com/spotlight/TheGrannysWritings
noniedoodles@yahoo.com

Love Never Dies in Harlequin's Inspirational Anthology, *A Kiss Under the Mistletoe*

Nonie's Big Bottom Girls' Rio Linda Cookbooks (4)

Nonie's Stuff" Cookbooks (Candy & Stuff* Cookies…&…Stuff* Soups & Stuff)*

Nosie Rosie's Diaries: (True cat diaries written by The Granny & The Windy) (Years 1 & 2 of 15-years so far)

noniedoodles color books (artwork by Nonie's original doodles) Several Volumes

Nonie's Cat Anthologies (Fun, not-so-fun and sometimes crazy short cat stories) 2 Volumes

Nonie's Wet Kitty Kisses Anthologies (Mostly humorous Short Stories…but NOT about cats) 2 Volumes

COYOTE POCKETS

PATRICIA E. CANTERBURY

"Christopher, I'm not going to tell you again, eat your breakfast."

"Yes, Mother." Christopher looked down at his bowl of strawberry-covered oats.

"It's your favorite. You've been moping around for a week."

"But Mother, I'm too excited to eat. It's only six weeks until the Ayers Elementary School's big field event and I want Coach to put me on the team."

"Honey, we've just moved here from Arizona. The coach hasn't had time to find out what sports you play."

"I know why he hasn't put me on the team. It's because I don't have pockets."

"Pockets, what are you talking about?"

"You know, pockets. Just last week when I spoke in front of the class about growing up in Arizona and how the sky was full of stars, even different stars from these down here in Australia, I told them about my best friends, Benjamin Bear and Rebecca Raccoon, but they didn't believe me. They said Benjamin couldn't have caught wild fish with his paws or eaten so many blueberries that he and I got sick. I told them how Rebecca and I would hunt at night, not a school night of course, and how well she saw at night. I told them that Rebecca knew the names of all the stars in Arizona."

"And what does Benjamin and Rebecca have to do with pockets?" Mother asked.

"All the kids were fascinated that I had a bear and a raccoon for friends, but they pointed and said American kids were funny 'cuz we don't have pockets." Christopher's eyes

115

filled with tears, which he immediately brushed away before his mother noticed. *I'm going to be 10 on the date of the big field event. I'm much too old to cry,* he thought.

"I'm the only one without pockets at school, except for the Hare triplets and the Rabbit twins, but they can hop and jump like all the other kids."

"Christopher, I don't know what I'm going to do with you. You don't need pockets. All of the kids love you. Here comes Kaitlin Kangaroo to walk to school with you."

Mother doesn't understand. I just know that I won't fit in until I have pockets just like all my Australian schoolmates.

"Hello, Mrs. Coyote, is Christopher ready for school?" Kaitlin asked as she walked into the kitchen.

"He'll be right out. He went to wash his face and brush his teeth. Christopher hasn't touched his breakfast. I don't know what's happening to him. Would you care for a glass of orange juice while you wait?"

"No, thank you, I'm stuffed."

"Hi Kaitlin, bye Mother." Christopher kissed his mother's cheek and took Kaitlin's paw as they began their walk to the school bus stop a block away.

* * *

"Christopher, meet me after school again, so we can practice your hopping steps. The Rabbit and Hare kids will be practicing so we will have company," Kaitlin said as she and Christopher shared a sandwich during lunch.

"Okay, maybe I'll learn something. The teacher told me that the Rabbit and Hare older brothers and sisters won all the blue ribbons for hopping/jumping at previous field events." *I'd like to win a blue ribbon for Mother and Father,* Christopher thought, *but I'll never win 'cuz I don't have pockets nor am I small like the Rabbits or Hares. The best athletes have pockets. I must get some pockets.*

* * *

"Coach Marsupial, let me run track," Christopher pleaded, a month before the field event.

"Track? I've never heard of track. I don't think I'd be any good in teaching you something I don't know. If you want to participate I'll teach you boxing."

"Thanks Coach, but I want to spend my time outside. I'll just work harder on learning to hop and jump."

* * *

"Pockets!" Father Coyote said.

"Yes dear. It's the only thing he asks for," Mother Coyote replied.

"Kids today," he said, shaking his head. "He gets his strange notions from your side of the family," Father joked, giving mother a hug.

"It's just a phase, dear. Remember a few years ago when all he spoke of was a train set?" Father continued, as he helped Mother wash the dinner dishes. "Now he hardly ever plays with it. Perhaps the kids here like pockets. I sure have noticed that almost everyone has one. We'll both listen more carefully and he'll tell us what he really wants, don't worry."

"Perhaps you're right. I'm worrying over nothing. I think he may like new running shoes. I saw him running in the field behind the house last week. He's always been an excellent runner."

* * *

After his conversation with Christopher, Coach Marsupial tried running around the high jump track. He was slow and clumsy. *Hump! Just as I thought, no one can run. It's not even a sport. I know sports; after all, I was the State Boxing Champion in college. I just need to coach my kids in what they do best, which is hopping and jumping. The new kid, Christopher, is a friendly, eager little coyote, but there isn't a place for him on the team.* Coach looked up from his seat near the grandstand just in time to see Christopher try one more time to jump the lowest hurdles. He fell and skinned his knees. He was terrible.

"It's okay, Christopher, we can't all be a pole vaulter or high jumpers. You can be my assistant and keep time," Coach said, as he put a small bandage on Christopher's knee and gave him a reassuring hug.

"But Coach, I want to run," Christopher said in a small voice too faint for Coach to hear.

"Did you say something?"

"I said thanks, Coach."

*   *   *

"Christopher, watch me. Do exactly what I do," Kaitlin called as she jumped over a small hurdle.

"Okay." Christopher did exactly what Kaitlin did, but he stumbled over his large feet.

"That's okay. You'll do better tomorrow," Kaitlin said.

"I can't jump. I'm too awkward. I don't have pockets," Christopher whined.

"There are lots of things you can do. You don't have to jump. We have many jumpers at school," Kaitlin replied, giving Christopher a sisterly hug.

*   *   *

"Good Morning, Christopher. Your birthday is only a few days away and Mother and I don't know what to get you for your first double digit day," Father said.

"I told you. I want pockets," Christopher replied softly.

"Here, sit down beside me. Look at the family photo album. See all the wonderful runners on both sides of our family? You should be happy with the gifts God gives you. You can run faster than any of the kids at school. You can also hunt better. You don't need to be a jumper for your mother and me to be proud of you. We love you just as you are."

"I know, Father, but there aren't any prizes for running. I want to fit in."

"Son, you do fit in. You have more friends than you had in Arizona. Everyone loves you."

"But..." Christopher hung his head. He knew his father was correct. He kissed his parents goodbye and ran to the school bus. It was true, he was an excellent runner.

* * *

It was finally November 26th, Christopher's tenth birthday, and the day of the big field competition.

"Remember dear, Father and I will meet you after the field events and we'll have ice cream and give you your present. Don't forget to take the basket of cookies to share with your class," Mother said, hugging Christopher goodbye.

* * *

"Look Christopher, the competition between Ayers' Rock and Queen Victoria's Mill always brings the entire town to the stadium. There's not an empty seat. The winner will represent Australia against New Zealand. Ayers' Rock has never won while Queen Victoria's Mill has gone to finals the last five years," Kaitlin said, as she straightened her purple and gold uniform for the girls' hurdles relay.

"Hello Mark, ready for today's competition?" Keith Kangaroo, the one-eyed coach from Queen Victoria's Mill said. He held the paw of a skinny dingo.

"Hello Keith. We're as ready as we're going to be. Who's that, your new jumper?" Coach Marsupial asked looking over at the dingo.

"Let me introduce you to Doug Dingo. He's my star pupil. We've entered him in the 100 meter dash. He can beat anyone you've got," Keith said with a sly grin.

"The 100 meter dash? What's that?" Coach Marsupial asked, but Keith and Doug had walked away.

"Coach...coach. I know about the 100 meter dash. We used to play it in Arizona. It's like running. I know I can win. Let me play...please?" Christopher asked.

"Where were you?" Coach asked, stunned by Christopher's excitement.

"I was behind the bleachers, but I heard everything Coach Kangaroo said. I know I can run faster than any ol' dingo."

"Okay, kid, let's see what you can do. Here's a jersey, number 10. Today's your tenth birthday, isn't it? Maybe this is your lucky day."

"I don't need pockets to beat any old dingo," Christopher said just loud enough for Doug to hear.

They stood at the start line, the starter gun went off. Christopher ran. He crossed the finish line before Doug reached the halfway mark. The crowd cheered. Christopher could barely hear himself think. He looked into the stadium, Kaitlin ran down to greet him, followed closely by his mother and father. Father gave him a bear hug just like Benjamin used to do. Mother handed him his present. Kaitlin kissed his cheek.

"Open your present before everyone gets here," Mother said. Christopher said a small prayer of thanks.

"Thank You for giving me strong, fast legs. I don't need pockets to be a winner." Christopher opened his present, inside was a beautiful handmade vest with four large pockets.

"You were right Mother and Father. I didn't need pockets to win. I just need my own God-given gifts," Christopher said, putting on his pocket vest.

 Patricia E. (Pat) Canterbury is a native of Sacramento, world traveler, philanthropist, art collector, political scientist, award-winning poet, short story contributor, author of *Every Thursday* and *The Geaha Incident*, adult mystery fiction, *Carlotta's Secret*, a children's mystery, as well as *The Secret of St. Gabriel's Tower*, *The Secret of Morton's End*, and *The Case of the Bent*

Spoke, pre-teen mystery novels in the *Poplar Cove Series*. Pat is also a poet and won the First Annual Georgia State Poetry Contest in 1987 for her collection, *Shadowdrifters...Images of China*. She has been fortunate to have published over 15 short stories in anthologies over the years. In addition to NCPA, Pat is a member of Capitol Crimes, MWA, SCBWI, and ZICA Creative Arts and Illustrators.

Visit her website or reach her at patmyst@aol.com or www.patmyst.com.

GREGORY

DOROTHY RICE

We found Gregory, a russet-toned guinea pig with unusually large eyes, at one of those "big box" pet stores, a high-ceilinged, cavernous emporium with aisle after aisle of merchandise. He was furtively rooting in the bedding at the bottom of a tall, rectangular cage that seemed intended for birds, rather than ground-dwelling creatures. When I knelt for a closer look, he backed into a purple plastic igloo and bugged his eyes at me. One of his ears hung limp. It was notched down the center as though it had been split and then healed. He had scratch marks on his muzzle where white skin showed through the brown fur.

I caught my husband Bob's eye and frowned. He grimaced back in unspoken agreement. This poor battle-scarred critter would not be coming home with us.

"How about some lunch?" I asked with forced cheeriness.

"I could eat," he said. "Burrito World?"

We both looked to Rose, our daughter, eleven at the time. Burrito World was her favorite. But she didn't seem to have heard. She'd slumped to the linoleum, feet tucked beneath her, fingers laced through the cage's metal bars.

"Can I hold him?" she asked.

"Really?" I said. "Maybe they have others."

"*Mom.*"

"What?"

"He can't help it," she said. "It's not his fault if he got in a fight."

There was a hitch in her voice and her eyes were bright with hope.

The clerk, a gangly young man with a weak chin, claimed

not to know anything about the brown guinea pig's personal history.

"I'm thinking he was sent over from another store," he said, which sounded vaguely ominous.

"What if he's a biter?" I said.

"*Mom.*"

"I wouldn't be able to return your money. But you can bring him back if he doesn't work out," the clerk said.

* * *

On the drive home, Rose sat in the back seat. A cardboard box with a handle and two rows of air holes rested on her lap.

"What's your name, little one?" she said, peering in at her new pet.

We both glanced at our youngest child in the rearview mirror. She was the last of five, the only one still at home.

* * *

Guinea pigs are naturally social creatures. That was why we'd been out shopping for another. Harold, our daughter's other pet, had recently lost his two cage mates, first Jelly Bean and then Skittles, with little warning, at least none that we'd noticed. We hoped Gregory would pull Harold out of his slump.

On a spring Saturday, not long after we brought Gregory home from the pet store, Rose was in the family room, setting up an obstacle course for the pigs' daily exercise regimen on the area rug that ran the length of the couch. She lifted segments of plastic pipe from their habitat and placed them in a zigzagged pattern from one end of the rug to the other. Gregory and Harold chattered and squeaked when she removed their plastic igloos to place at either end of the course.

A quarter of the family room, cordoned off with a low wire fence, was given up to the pig habitat. We'd lined the floor with plastic sheeting and towels, and liberally sprinkled the area with fresh hay. As a result, the house smelled like a barn.

Rose's three guinea pigs used to roam the structure freely, but since Gregory, the cage had been split down the middle. He hadn't hurt Harold, but the clucking and teeth chattering and the way he sidled around the smaller pig, nipping and flicking his nose in the air, was worrisome.

Rose snapped carrots into chunks and set them between the segments of pipe to lure the pigs from one end of the course to the other.

"Your turn first," she said, lifting Harold from his side of the cage. He inched his nose forward and stretched out to full length before venturing into the first segment of black pipe and capturing the carrot at the other end.

"Good job," Rose said, as he chewed industriously.

Sponge Bob yammered in the background on the television as I loaded the dishwasher.

"Hey, sweetie," I said. "It's a beautiful day. How about you call Susie. You girls could ride bikes to the park or something. I could pack you a picnic."

She didn't look up.

"*Rose.*"

"I'm busy Mom."

"Susie had you over. It's our turn."

"*Right.*"

I'd had to work late the prior week and asked Susie's mother if she could keep our daughter after basketball practice. Bob could have picked her up, but it was a chance for the girls to spend more time together. Rose hadn't had a good friend, a "real" friend, since fourth grade.

She started Gregory on the course. Harold sniffed the carpet, snuffling up tiny bits of ground carrot that had fallen from his mouth. The two pigs seemed to pay no attention to one another.

"You have to make an effort if you want to make friends," I said.

Rose crossed her arms over her chest.

"Maybe I don't want to," she said.

Harold scrabbled across the wood laminate flooring and darted under the couch. Gregory sniffed the air and took off after him, his body an elongated brown streak. Harold screeched and dug frantically at the floor as Gregory cornered him. Rose flung herself down on her belly and thrust her arm under the couch. She let out a yelp then pulled her arm back out. We both stared at her bloodied fingertip.

I grabbed the broom from the kitchen cupboard and swished it beneath the couch. When Harold darted out, I scooped him up and set him back in the cage.

Rose captured Gregory and held him close, his nose just beneath her chin. "It's okay, little one. I know you didn't mean it."

She smoothed Gregory's fur until his frantic chattering became a guttural, trilling sound. When she returned him to the cage, Gregory crossed to the fence that separated him from Harold. The two pigs sidled close to one another so that the lengths of their bodies touched through the wire mesh. Harold fluffed out his hair and cooed. Gregory responded with his throaty trill.

"See, they love each other," she said, more to herself than to me. "Gregory just gets scared."

I fetched a band-aid and some Neosporin© from the hall cupboard. Sitting beside Rose on the couch, I swabbed and wrapped her fingertip tight.

* * *

The summer before Rose started high school, she found Harold on his side. His four little feet formed two x's on the cage floor, as though he'd been trotting in his sleep. After a burial ceremony in the backyard, she retreated to her room and closed the door. When I tiptoed upstairs to let her know dinner was ready, she stirred from a fetal ball to pull the covers up over her head.

Downstairs, Bob and I kept the TV off and listened for her steps on the stairs. The big house echoed with her absence.

"No more," I said. "Gregory is the last one. Ever."

*　*　*

Gregory began to lose weight, seemingly going the way of Skittles, Jelly Bean and Harold, who'd all reached a point where they lost interest in food. Like the others, we took him to the veterinary clinic near our house.

"Guinea pigs are like cows. They eat continuously," the vet said. "Once the stomach loses its *prime* there isn't much you can do. Try to tempt him with his favorite foods."

A matter-of-fact woman of late middle age, she gave us a concentrated high-nutrition green food. Per her instructions, we mixed the pungent powder with water to form a mash and attempted to feed Gregory with a baby spoon. When that proved fruitless, we experimented with a liquid medicine dropper. Aside from not eating, Gregory was alert and active. I asked the vet if there wasn't something else that could be done for him. She suggested we find a practice that specialized in "exotics," a category that encompassed smaller mammals, birds and lizards.

The animal hospital, where we brought Gregory next, boasted several vets with small mammal expertise. An earnest young vet with thick glasses in black frames palpated the pig's skin. She stretched it between her fingers and said he was badly dehydrated.

Gregory was admitted to the hospital, hooked up to intravenous fluids and fed the concentrated green mash every four hours. The expenses mounted. But we'd determined to do whatever we could for him.

After four days in the hospital, the bespectacled vet was cautiously hopeful. Gregory was hydrated, taking the food well, and he'd begun to poop again.

"That's huge," the vet said, poking at a poop pellet with her fingertip. "The trick is to get the system moving again." She gave us instructions for maintaining the rigorous feeding schedule and for monitoring his stool, both for quantity and shape—sickly pig pellets resemble broken chromosomes rather than uniformly shaped lozenges.

*   *   *

The first night shift was mine. When the alarm buzzed at 2:00 am, I slipped into my robe and set up the guinea pig feeding station on the couch—six plastic syringes filled with green super food nestled in a bowl, and several towels. I swaddled Gregory like a baby, only his head sticking out, held him with one hand, and slowly pressed the plunger into a corner of his mouth, allowing him time to gulp and swallow.

I had assumed Gregory would claw and struggle. Yet once I'd mastered the technique, his small body went limp beneath the towel. His tiny hands were still and his big, brown eyes never left mine. After I emptied each syringe, I wiped his muzzle clean with a damp washcloth. In the quiet, darkened house, the tick of the clock and the scrape of the syringe on the bowl the only sounds, I willed life into his twenty ounces of ragged skin, bone and fur.

After a few days, Gregory was greedily sucking down his green food but still unable or unwilling to eat on his own. Though we'd vowed no more guinea pigs, Bob and I decided that if having a companion could make the difference, it was worth a try.

The three of us visited the humane society that Saturday. We'd called ahead and knew there were three adolescent brothers left from a litter. They were white with pink eyes and varying patterns of orange splotches. A tattooed and pierced volunteer brought them to us in one of the visitation rooms. We sat on the floor, gave the guinea pig brothers their freedom, and observed as they followed one another nose to tail, snuffling tufts of animal hair that swirled in the corners. One of the three broke away from the others to sniff Rose's pants leg. He didn't skitter back to the pack when she stroked his back.

Rose named him Marmalade Jam.

We brought Marmalade home. Bob set him down in the side of the cage that had been Harold's. We breathed a sigh of relief when Gregory sidled up to the fence between them and settled there, seeming to find comfort in the closeness.

* * *

Even with his new companion, it was clear Gregory was not yet on the mend. He stuck beside Marmalade, yet still wasn't eating on his own. After a middle of the night feeding, I opened my laptop.

I searched websites dedicated to guinea pig care. Numerous explanations for loss of appetite were offered—stress, infection, dietary and environmental changes. None seemed to apply to any of the four guinea pigs we'd watched languish and die.

Clicking and scrolling through more sites, I stumbled on "malocclusion," a condition where the guinea pig's teeth, which continue to grow throughout their life, have overgrown to the extent that they trap the tongue and prevent the pig from chewing and swallowing. There were graphic photographs of guinea pig mouths stretched wide, and of the surgical clamps and clippers used to correct the condition.

I swaddled Gregory, held him under the light, delicately inserted a finger into either side of his mouth to part his black lips, and peered inside. His tongue was thick and humped up, trapped by his teeth. Gregory wasn't lonely, stressed or anorexic. Eating was a physical impossibility. I wondered if it had been the same for the others. Shaky with anger and frustration at what we'd put him through, hospitalization and days of pointless, hand feeding, I waited for morning to call the "experts" at the animal hospital.

I took Gregory back to the vet's office. After a quick look inside his mouth, the vet confirmed my diagnosis. Gregory was admitted for surgery.

* * *

A few days after the operation, Gregory was back home, recuperating. He'd seemed to rally and even nibbled some lettuce.

Rose and I were out shopping when my cell phone rang. It was Bob. Rose searched my face, and though I said nothing and thought I'd kept my expression blank, she knew. Gregory had died.

Likely the surgery came too late or perhaps the trauma was too much for him.

* * *

Rose was now in high school. It wouldn't be long before she goes off to college.

One evening, the first week back at school after winter break, Rose allowed herself a breather from homework. We sat beside one another on the couch, watching television. Marmalade was an orange and white lump on her chest.

"Did you hear from Kathy at all during the break?" I asked.

Kathy is her current "best" friend, a girl she eats lunch with every day and sees in classes but whom she rarely hears from outside of school.

"Whatever," Rose said, with a shrug. "We texted at Christmas and New Year's. I'm over it. She is what she is."

She ruffled Marmalade's fur and leaned her head on my shoulder.

"It's not that I want to be popular or anything," she said. "I just think it would be nice to have a real friend, someone that wants to talk to me, to be with me, you know, on their own, without me always initiating it. That's a thing, isn't it?"

* * *

We have learned a few things from eight years of guinea pig husbandry.

Rose is diligent in feeding Marmalade mainly roughage,

plenty of hay, to keep his teeth ground down. And should he stop munching, should he excrete a misshapen pellet, we'll know to look inside his tiny mouth for answers.

Marmalade is not so physically commanding as Gregory. He stays where he's set, stares with pink piggy eyes, munches carrots and hay with stolid determination and makes endearing noises when he's petted. Yet even he, a mostly inert ball of fur, has taught us what Rose knew all along.

What matters most is being there.

Dorothy Rice is the author of *The Reluctant Artist*, an art book/memoir published by Shanti Arts in October 2015. *Gray Is the New Black*, a memoir of ageism, sexism and self-acceptance, was published by *Otis Books* in June 2019. After raising five children and retiring from a career in environmental protection, Rice earned an MFA in Creative Writing from UC Riverside, Palm Desert, at 60. Her essays and stories have been widely published in journals and magazines. A San Francisco native, Dorothy is a long-time Sacramento resident. Learn more at www.dorothyriceauthor.com and follow Dorothy on twitter @dorothyrowena.

A GIFT FOR GRANDMA

RACHEL CHU

"Wait, Grandma's turning 70?" Robin exclaimed while scrolling through her phone notifications.

It was the first week of January, the last Friday of break before school was to start. Robin was in the middle of her freshman year of high school.

"I thought she was turning 70 next year." Haley quickly glanced over at Robin before turning her focus back to the road. Haley, Robin's artsy, imaginative older sister, was graduating from high school.

"No, it's definitely this year." Robin leaned her head on the passenger side door as she looked at Haley in the driver's seat. They were both a bit sore from an afternoon of ice skating.

"What are we going to do?" Haley shot a nervous grin at her usually placid sister.

Robin decided that the best course of action was to consult her most trusted confidant. "Siri, what should I get my grandma for her birthday?"

"But, Robin, we don't want her to think we forgot her birthday."

Siri responded, "Sorry, I didn't quite get that. Please repeat."

"Ah, never mind, Siri." Robin put her phone down.

Haley ran her fingers through her long, dark locks.

"Okay, what can we bring?" Robin breathed deeply through her nose.

"What about a bouquet of flowers?" suggested Haley.

"That's so inadequate. Here, Grandma, some pitiful flowers. Seven decades old and all we got you were some

131

grocery store flowers because we forgot that today was your birthday?" Robin shook her head.

"It isn't that bad. And we didn't forget really. We still got a day." Haley widened her eyes.

Robin pursed her lips and made a barely audible groan. "That's what we're trying to avoid. We're such bad grandchildren."

As they continued to deliberate, they came to a stop sign where they waited for a pedestrian to cross the street.

"Hold up. Are you thinking what I'm thinking?" Haley grinned impishly.

"I'm thinking about getting her a box of fancy donuts." Robin pointed to the neighborhood donut shop that just opened.

"No, are you kidding?" Haley threw her head forward.

"What? You're being dramatic."

"A dog, Robin, a dog. We should get Grandma a dog." Haley pointed to the lady walking her dog across the street.

"Ohhh." Robin raised her hand to her forehead as Haley lifted her foot from the brake pedal. "Wait, say what? Where are we going to find a dog?"

"Oh, I don't know. Maybe this wasn't such a great idea."

"You said it."

"Oh, Robin. I got it. Our neighbor's chihuahua just had puppies a few weeks ago."

"Mr. Lee is a pretty stern guy."

"Nah, he's nice."

"And, Haley, dogs are dirty. And you can't possibly expect Grandma to clean up after a dog."

"Yeah, but dogs are good companions."

"Dogs just seem like so much work, especially for a 70-year-old grandma."

"I just know Grandma will love it."

"I don't know about that."

The sisters pulled into the driveway.

Haley jumped out of the car. "Let's go to Mr. Lee's house to see if he still has the puppies."

"Mom, Dad, we're going to Mr. Lee's to get a puppy." Haley poked her head around to the back porch.

"Haley Nella, what do you think you are doing? You know our landlord doesn't allow pets," Haley and Robin's mother, Meg, stated flatly.

"Not for me, for Grandma. Come with."

"For my mother?" Haley and Robin's father, Tony, questioned. "Wait, we're coming."

Haley and Robin darted across the front lawn to Mr. Lee's house. "Mr. Lee, we'd like to have a puppy if you still have them."

"Sorry, ladies. I only have the runt left."

The dog heard himself being called a runt again, and he didn't like it but he knew it was true. He wasn't quite as big or perfect as his big sisters and brothers.

"Runt is good. We'll take the runt," Haley quickly responded.

A bit taken aback, Mr. Lee invited the family in. "Have a seat. Wait just a moment."

The dog was a bit surprised too and opened his eyes a bit wider.

"Oh, won't you look at those puppy eyes." Tony's eyes crinkled and a smile started to form across his face.

The dog knew the eye trick his older brothers had taught him was working.

"Yeah, I actually think your mom will like that." Meg looked at Tony and grinned.

"Here you go." Mr. Lee handed the puppy to Robin.

"I like it. Let's get it. How much will you charge, Mr. Lee?"

"Wait, I'm not so sure about this." Trepidation was written across Haley's face. "Maybe this wasn't such a great idea after all."

"Oh, come on, the puppy is perfect. You were so right." Robin gently passed the little puppy over to Haley, who sat straight up, tensing as she attempted to hold the puppy gently.

The puppy knew he had to win Haley over, so he nested his soft nose into her elbow.

Mr. Lee watched Haley bond with the puppy and thought for a moment. "If you want him, you can have him. No charge for you. I'm going to Europe for a month, so if you can watch my house for me while I'm gone, that will be adequate payment."

"Done," Robin responded before anyone in her family had a chance.

As the puppy cradled its head in Haley's elbow, Haley smiled. "Yeah. Grandma will love him."

Early the next morning, Tony and Meg were in the front seat, and Haley and Robin carried a big red box in the backseat of the car all the way to Tony's parents' house. The inside of the box was lined with blankets and had a small bowl of food.

The dog didn't like the dark, cold box, but all he could do was whimper. And from the outside, it just seemed like the box whimpered.

When they arrived, Haley carried the suspicious box to the front door. Joe, Tony's father and Haley and Robin's grandfather, opened the door for the family and smirked when he saw the big red box with an oversized bow and little holes all over. "Grandma's in the living room," he whispered.

"Happy Birthday!"

Charlotte went for a round of hugs before picking up the box. She nervously untied the ribbon and stepped back for a moment when she heard a whimper coming from it.

She carefully removed the lid. Everyone in the room knew that it was love at first bark.

Charlotte squealed a high pitch squeal of excitement and she reached into the box to pet her furry new friend. "Yahoo! I can't believe you got me a puppy. I love you, Haley and Robin. Oh, and of course I love you two too," she said as she turned to Meg and Tony.

And just then, his name was decided. The little puppy, the runt of the litter, was affectionately named *Yahoo*.

Charlotte picked Yahoo up out of the red box and looked over at Joe. "Can you believe it? They got me a puppy."

And just then, Joe's smile stretched into a grimace. "Are

you sure about this? Can we handle a puppy? You're seventy!"

"Oh, I know how old I am. Live a little, Joe."

"If you say so," Joe muttered under his breath. His uneasiness was perceptible to his son, Tony, who quickly spoke up.

"Dad, can we go outside for a moment?"

Joe and Tony walked to the sliding door leading to the backyard.

"I'm not so sure about this," Joe whispered.

"I know it'll take some time to get used to, but I'm sure you'll come to love...what's she calling it, Yahoo?"

"I guess. Couldn't you guys give me some warning?"

"Now, where's the fun in that?"

"Well, I love you anyways, son."

"I know. I love you too, Dad." The two fellas walked back inside.

"Oh, lookie here. Yahoo wants to say hello to you, Joe."

Yahoo smiled as big as he could and showed all his little teeth. He wholeheartedly believed Joe would love him someday even if it wasn't today.

Charlotte waved the little puppy's hand and squeaked on behalf of the dog. "Hello, Joe. You're gonna love me, Joe."

"Oh, I know I will." Joe walked over to Charlotte and picked up the puppy from her. As he held the puppy, some might even call it puppy love, took over.

Yahoo was satisfied. He realized he had the power to melt hearts. He liked this new family.

"What do we feed this dog-kid of mine?" Charlotte asked her granddaughters.

"Dog food, I guess? We didn't really think this through, did we?" Haley giggled while glancing at Robin.

As Meg and Tony walked to the kitchen to prepare lunch, Joe and Charlotte walked to the backyard with Haley and Robin who were now playing with Yahoo.

"Yahoo is just too cute! Thank you, girls." Charlotte held Yahoo and smiled at her granddaughters.

Yahoo liked his new home. Everyone was so nice and

complimentary.

"You're very welcome. Happy Birthday, Grandma!" Haley spoke on behalf of the sisters.

Before long, lunch was ready, and Meg and Tony brought the sandwiches out to the patio.

"Well, I guess Yahoo can just share with me." Charlotte smirked as she stuck a little piece of bread into Yahoo's mouth. Yahoo howled with joy in response.

It was the best food Yahoo had ever tasted in his young life.

"I think he likes that," Joe noted.

You bet I do, Yahoo thought to himself.

"Let's see if he's a picky eater." Charlotte took a small piece of lettuce from her sandwich and fed it to Yahoo, who quickly licked it off her hand.

Yahoo liked that even better.

When Charlotte tried feeding Yahoo a small corner of her roast beef, he licked ferociously as if licking would cause more meat to show up.

Yahoo hoped that every meal would have meat as good as that roast beef.

The family enjoyed their time together and soon it was time for Tony, Meg, and the girls to go home.

"See you soon, Grandma and Grandpa!" The girls gave Charlotte a hug, then Joe, and then Yahoo.

"Be good, Yahoo!" Robin whispered to Yahoo as she walked out the door.

Yahoo howled in agreement.

"What are we going to do with this dog?" Joe asked Charlotte, who had held Yahoo all evening.

"I'll get him a blanket for him to go to sleep." Charlotte walked into the hallway closet and brought out a brand-new blanket she got from her most recent Secret Santa gift exchange.

The next morning, Joe and Charlotte woke up to a shredded blanket on their living room floor and no dog to be found.

"Oh, no! Where's Yahoo?" Charlotte shrieked.

"Oh, look at this mess!" Joe responded in contrast.

Charlotte looked in every nook and cranny of the living room, then the kitchen, then the bathroom, then the guest room, and then outside. Yahoo was nowhere to be found. In the meantime, Joe cleaned up the blanket shreds and tried to salvage some larger pieces while he put most of it in the trash.

"Oh, what a waste of a perfectly good blanket." Charlotte sighed and looked at Joe in despair.

"It's okay. Let's just focus on finding Yahoo," Joe said calmly as he looked at Charlotte.

Joe and Charlotte walked outside and started to walk down the neighborhood. "Yahoo, where are you, come back!" Charlotte called out to the street with tears in her eyes.

Unbeknownst to the grandparents, Yahoo was enjoying a nice nap under Joe and Charlotte's bed.

Charlotte and Joe walked the whole neighborhood before Joe finally spoke up, "Yahoo isn't here. We should go home now."

It was mid-morning, and Joe and Charlotte hadn't eaten breakfast yet. They walked home quietly. When they got home, Joe made some scrambled eggs, while Charlotte made one more round in the backyard.

"Yahoo was the best dog ever," Charlotte said aloud.

"Even though you only had him for a day," Joe responded in agreement as Charlotte walked into the house.

Yahoo could hear his name and his ears perked up. He liked his new name. In fact, in all the conversation he overheard in the past day, he learned that his new owner's best friend's dog was named Google. Yahoo was excited to meet Google, a male, two-year-old poodle. As the morning light moved towards noon, the sun was no longer hitting Yahoo in his little alcove under the bed, so Yahoo moved a little forward to where the sunlight hit the ground in the room. Then, Yahoo heard Charlotte crying softly in the other room.

"Oh, what am I gonna tell the girls?" Charlotte sobbed in

reference to Haley and Robin, who got her the best birthday present ever.

Joe put his arm around Charlotte. "It will be okay." They ate their breakfast more quietly than usual.

Yahoo got a little sad that Charlotte thought he was gone for good. And he frowned and breathed heavily through his nostrils, but his spot was too comfortable and he didn't want to get in trouble for the shredded blanket, so he stayed where he was. Yahoo was getting a little hungry, but he decided it was more important to be comfortable for now. Besides, Joe and Charlotte could just walk into their room and see him resting on the floor.

Charlotte got up, put her plate in the sink, and sat down on the couch.

"Well, I have an idea," Joe said with a smirk.

"Do tell!" Charlotte motioned for him to keep talking

At the same time, Yahoo's ears perked up.

"Well, we could go to the pet store and get a new chihuahua and name him Yahoo. The girls would never have to know."

"Are you kidding?" Charlotte said in disbelief.

"Not at all," Joe joked. "This could actually work."

Yahoo did not like the sound of Joe's plan at all. He did not like that his new owners would so easily give up and just go buy another dog to replace him. He thought they would keep searching and eventually find him, but they were already talking about replacing him. Yahoo knew he was irreplaceable, but clearly his new owners didn't understand that. Yahoo was offended and disappointed. After his long morning bask in the sunlight, he stood up on all four legs and marched like a proud dog into the living room where Charlotte and Joe sat.

"YAHOO!" Charlotte squealed.

"Where were you, little dog?" Joe said in a surprised voice.

Yahoo only responded with a quiet bark.

Charlotte picked up Yahoo. "We'll be better dog parents, I promise. And Yahoo, I want you to remember one thing, you're irreplaceable."

And while Yahoo wasn't so sure about the first part of her statement, he was pretty sure the latter part was true and he licked her face in agreement.

Yahoo, Charlotte, and Joe became best of friends and they lived happily ever after.

Rachel Chu is a college student in Northern California, studying Marketing and International Business. She has been a member of the NCPA since 2016. Rachel has previously co-authored a children's book, *A Trip to the Moon*. Chu enjoys spending time with family, playing a competitive board game, eating dessert, watching a riveting medical drama, or traveling the country.

TEX'S DREAM

CAROLYN RADMANOVICH

L ife was good until the day Turk arrived at our house. It was hate at first sight. He was bumbling and drooly, and most of all he was a d-d-d-dog. I hate dogs. Always have. Mother Cat told me, "Tex, watch out for those hairy beasts for they may chew you up for breakfast."

Not only did Turk bark at me, but he nipped at my legs when I ran. Each day that went by, I was sure he had grown a couple of inches and his teeth grew with him into nightmarish, long fangs. Every day, his enthusiasm to catch me and my determination to escape, escalated.

My family was sweet and loving, but how could they possibly get a d-d-d-dog when they had a magnificent cat such as myself? I felt betrayed.

I took my time planning my escape. I couldn't allow my new family to own a dog, which left out about half the neighbors as candidates, so I decided to do some sleuthing research.

One family had four boys, and they spent the day pounding a ball and knocking it against the wall of their garage into this hoop thing. They would become excited if it slid through nice and easy. Stupid game, but they loved it. If I lived there, I'd probably get pounded by the ball or smashed by scurrying feet, so I eliminated them from my list.

A bachelor lived in the house next door, but he was always off hiking or biking in West Africa or sailing the South Seas. That wouldn't do. When I felt like napping or cuddling, I needed a nice warm lap.

I loved the two girls in the house at the end of the street, but when I would go over to visit and get petted, they kept talking about getting a Doberman Pincer. I'd never be able to outrun one of those. Turk was bad enough, but I'd be a goner the first day they brought home that cat-hater.

I made my rounds, climbing fences and checking the various scents in people's yards. I ran into an old orange warrior-cat, Baxter. He refused to allow a cat to walk on his lawn, sniff his flowers, or walk on the fence highway bordering his house. I knew when I wasn't wanted, but decided to check on him from time-to-time.

One day Baxter's servant ambled to the mailbox and I followed her. She bent down and petted me in that special way only cat lovers know. I got scratched behind the ears, my back, under the chin, and patted on my head. Boy, was Baxter lucky. For me, it was love at first sight. I accompanied the woman home and rubbed against her legs to let her know I was interested if there were any vacancies pending.

You never knew what the future held for this old guy, Baxter. Maybe he didn't see so well because he was geriatric and maybe he'd attempt to have a romantic liaison with a skunk and get smoked. Like any self-respecting cat, he'd be humiliated and run away from home, never to return. Baxter might nap under the wheels of his owner's car and because he didn't hear so well, he wouldn't know when she started up her car, and he'd get squashed. Worst of all, there was a possibility he could flop over from excessive fleas. There are grave dangers in being an aging cat.

I decided to bide my time between keeping out of sight when Turk was around and lurking by the mailbox to see if Baxter's owner was looking for those funny papers they liked to receive. I made nice to the owner and found by listening to her talk to her man-friend that her name was Sandy. They became excited when I greeted them and rubbed on their legs. They laughed and petted me and said how handsome I was. Not that compliments affect me, but I could never get enough of them. Handsome, was I?

One brisk day, I jumped the fence to see if Baxter was around. He walked with a limp and spent his time bathing and

141

then sunning himself to dry. He slept a lot. He still hollered and howled when he saw me, but didn't bother getting up to chase me. This was my sign.

The rainy days came and I didn't venture out as much. I stayed upstairs in my house to be safe and to make sure Turk didn't use me as a chew toy. He was full-grown now and never overcame his passion for chasing me. How could my owners stand to be around a bumbling lout? In my mind, Turk had no lovable qualities. He dropped fur throughout the house and chewed the owner's shoes. I may drop fur from time-to-time, but I would never dream of chewing shoes. Cats are such superior creatures in every way. They have no ego, are independent and quite smart.

When the rain let up, I sauntered over to Baxter's house, and he didn't come out to howl at me. I sniffed around the yard and the rain had washed away any scent. I searched the flower bed and found a large pile of rocks. My heart went crazy. I was sad, but happy at the same time. My old buddy, Baxter, had gone on to the happy mousing grounds and had been buried here in his favorite garden.

Sandy stood with her back to me, watering plants. When she finished, I rushed up to her, meowing to let her know how sorry I was for her loss and to extend my condolences. She became teary when she saw me and crouched down to pet me. I jumped in her lap, knocking her over and she laughed.

When Sandy walked to the back door of the house, I jammed my way past her legs and into the kitchen. She laughed again. Good sign.

Sandy's man-friend picked up a box of cat snacks and shook it. I meowed in my excitement. My favorite cat snacks. How did he know?

After I finished eating, I noticed Sandy sitting on a chair. I dashed over and sat on her lap, making happy-paws and kneading her legs. When she responded with her super special strokes across my back, I sang my best purring song I learned from my mother.

Yes, my fondest dream has come true. I am in love and

happy. There are no dogs here, no howling cats, and two people who adore me. What more is there to life than this? Life is extraordinary.

Fascinated by the wild west, Carolyn Radmanovich earned a history degree from San Jose State University. After a near-drowning incident on the Russian River, she felt compelled to write her first book, *The Shape-Shifter's Wife*, about an anthropologist who time travels to the 1848 California gold rush and meets a handsome Frenchman. The sequel, *The Gypsy Palm Reader's Warning*, is Carolyn's current project. She belongs to the NCPA, The California Writers Club, and participates in a Critique Group with the EGWA. *The Shape-Shifter's Wife* won the 2018 Independent Book Awards for Visionary Fiction.

CATOPIAN DREAMS

ROBERTA L. DAVIS

Wasteland-themed movies had nothing on this place. Ashes coated the land, half-melted, twisted piles of vehicles, decimated buildings, everything. After extreme heat came the harshness of winter. Biting wind, scavengers, and rain unearthed ruined bits of past lives, junk mixed amidst tiny treasures that would succumb to floods and mudslides. The whole town was hazardous now. One never knew when a burned tree would tip over or a charred building would collapse. Those left behind, mostly cats, shivered through the long, gloomy days, bellies rumbling as their tender feet trod upon the landscape of ruin, hunting for food, shelter, any relief, well, almost any relief.

"RUN!"

A couple of cats huddling together for warmth bolted out from an old fireplace, running until they realized it was just Schitzy again. Schitzy-cat was one of many who were always on the lookout. She moved better than the others, for her paws fared better than most. Her disheveled fur ruffled in the cold wind. None of them wanted to lick each other. Everything tasted bad here, even their fur.

"Dang it, Schitzy-girl, what's wrong this time?" a Russian Blue hissed.

Schitzy's ears twitched as she sat back down, wrapping her tail around herself. As with many cats in the charred zone, she had some damage to the edges of her delicate ears. Likewise, her whiskers had been scorched short from the flash of hell they'd lived through, and varying stages of burns or worn pads made their paws highly tender.

"I think I was dreaming," she muttered.

Grumbling, the other cats shrugged off the scare as another false warning.

A large, black cat lumbered into view, his movements bored. One ear tip was missing from long ago, when he was equally naïve. Nacht, as humans called him, was a rare feral. He graduated from a scrapping barn cat to a pampered indoor guy. He remembered both sides of life. His calm demeanor soothed the others a bit as he strutted across a scattering of wreckage. Nacht crouched inside a modified crate that protected some food and fresh water. He stuck his face into the food bowl. "You kids are gonna starve if you don't suck it up," he warned between chomps. "Come eat."

Schitzy and two muddy tabbies smelled the kibbles along with scents of strange humans. They chowed down, but not for long. The stench of smoke polluted the air, while mystery chemicals tainted the ground. A gust of wind overturned nearby debris, sending the tabbies running. One gray tabby had a swagger from a limp, while the brown tabby was so nervous, he stuttered while meowing. Swatter and Stutters darted off towards one of the many junk piles.

"Amateurs," Nacht huffed.

"Aren't you scared?" Schitzy asked, glancing nervously around. Her long, multi-colored fur was missing in patches, giving her the illusion of having more spots.

"No, you've never been outside," Nacht surmised. "What's your real name?"

Schitzy timidly eased closer, so slowly that it might take all day. "I'm Amelia, and no, I haven't! There used to be birds outside the window. I'd lay and watch them, and my people were good to me! I had it all – treats, hugs, beds, toys everywhere. Why'd they leave us?" she yowled, a high-pitched, piteous noise. "How could they abandon me?"

Nacht hopped on top of the food bin and started licking himself, stopping after a few foul-tasting moments of grooming. He remembered the good life – naps by a fireplace that didn't set the world aflame, treats, toys, and soft beds. Before that, he lived the wild life outside of homes, but never was his outside life this bad. At least then, he had a barn and warm straw to sleep in, when he wasn't ridding his family's farm of vermin. "Humans are hard to rely on, well, most of them. But this time, it's different. Everyone left everyone when the fire-demon struck."

The sound of howling carried over the wind. Amelia charged into the feeding station, one foot landing in the food dish, scattering the kibbles. She peeked out with wide, copper-colored eyes. "What was that?"

Nacht hackled up, tail lashing. "Coyotes. That's what you should really fear. They're far worse than dogs, always hungry. You'd be a great snack, a healthy, tender, fluffball. I know where there's more chow. Come on."

Thunder rumbled from the sky. Rain pelted them, making them seek shelter. Nacht led Amelia to another feeding station in what was left of an alley. After that, he led her to a homemade feral cat house made from a big, plastic bin with straw inside.

Days passed without many visitors except other cats and a few roaming coyotes, and humans. Some cats witnessed humans setting out bowls of food and water in makeshift cubbies. Most cats thought it magically arrived. Sometimes human workers would manage to catch a cat, or at least, share a meal. A tenuous coexistence began to develop. Soon, the braver strays began waiting near work sites for breakfast. Sometimes, a really lucky cat went home with a sweet-talking stranger.

More humans showed up, but few stayed nearby. Many were workers, toiling for long hours in the muck of the ruins. The humans rounded up many animals – horses, cows, dogs, even a few parrots and other loose pets. They quickly realized that it was very hard to herd cats. So trappers took over, searching in the night, mostly ladies who talked nicely and left yummy food.

Days turned into weeks. Amelia discovered snow, fascinating, yet frigid. While the other cats had snow-paw fights, she tiptoed in the white stuff, pawed at it, left her territorial marking, and escaped to their dry cubby. Nacht taught her the ways of feral cats. Amelia learned when to hide from danger and huddle in a small, dry place to retain body heat. She found out how to hunt for real, to savor a rare bird or mouse between feedings left from humans. The first hunt was her hardest. Amelia took great delight in pouncing at a group of birds who were pecking at a worker's lunch scraps. Every bird escaped.

A week later, she and Nacht captured a mouse. Amelia batted it around gleefully, almost losing it. Each time the mouse almost escaped, Nacht batted it back into play.

Weary of the game, he dryly informed, "You have to kill it, like so." He lunged for it.

Aghast, Amelia saw her first rodent carnage that day. After barely nibbling on the juicy prey, she went for the feeding station of dry food instead as Nacht covered his face with his paws.

While she grudgingly accepted her predator instincts, Amelia missed her home, her family. She didn't dare approach strangers, not even when they had food. Memories of her warm, cozy, home faded in the waking hours, but returned in her sleep, letting her relive happy days where she felt safe and loved. She woke up snuggled against Nacht on a bitterly cold morning. A thin layer of frost covered everything outside their cubby. As she stretched for a better look through the tiny shelter's doorway, her stirring awoke Nacht.

"Stay put," he mumbled, "bad things out there."

"Why don't we go visit my home? I know where it is, uh, where it used to be."

"Humans aren't like us. They hardly ever come back," he said quietly.

She stared at him in dismay. "How can you say that?"

"Oh, kiddo," Nacht rolled his eyes before curling up closer to her, "you dream a lot. Let's say they try to find you. They're not good hunters. Why do you think I caught the mice for them?"

One night, one of those twig forts showed up closer than

usual to their feeding station. Tantalizing smells of dinner drew them closer to odd little cubbies, like straight twigs woven together, only much harder than wood, with a doorway at one end. Wonderful wet food lay in a container at the closed end of the twig house.

While Nacht lingered behind and kept watch, Amelia fell for the irresistible kibbles. Into the trap she snuck. *Wow, turkey bits!* She scarfed the meal, memories rushing back of warm food, sweet words, and cuddle time, until the door behind her slammed shut.

Amelia lurched forward, banging her head on the trap. "OW!" She freaked out, caterwauling and clawing at the walls. "MEEOWW! Nacht! Why didn't you warn me? You must've known—you know everything! What the *#*@(#?!"

Nacht rubbed his head against the cage, tail swishing. "You'll thank me later." He trotted away and vanished into the shadows. He turned to watch, only his green, blinking eyes barely visible in the approaching light.

A soft-spoken woman came and put a towel over Amelia's fort of entrapment. Talking nicely, the woman carried Amelia away.

Nacht hopped onto a charred log to watch his friend vanish into a vehicle. He would miss her, but he had others to look after. "Good luck, Kid."

Roberta "Bert" Davis has written fantasy and science fiction since childhood. She's a former Air Reserve Technician and retired from the USAF Reserves as Master Sergeant after twenty-two years of service. A graduate of ERAU (Embry-Riddle Aeronautical University), her thesis was on Human Factors in Aircraft Maintenance. She works as a lead technical writer by day, and writes sci-fi/fan by night. Roberta's first novel is in final edits by her and her editor (should be named the "100 Year Book" for taking so long).

She's published in the first two anthologies of SSWC (Sacramento Suburban Writer's Club): *The Moving Finger Writes* and *Thinking Through Our Fingers*. Roberta is a lifelong animal enthusiast, learning from trainers and behaviorists much of her life. She volunteers some hours to Fieldhaven Feline Rescue and is a staunch supporter of animal and wildlife rescue. Her Facebook is www.facebook.com/Dragonscriber.

THE CAT IS ALWAYS RIGHT

ELLEN OSBORN

I am a cat. My earliest memories are of playing with my brothers and sister and snuggling next to our mother. Then came a day when some strangers visited our house. They played with me and my brothers and sister. When they left they took one of my brothers! Did our lady know that she had let cat-nappers into our cozy home? Well really, I didn't miss that brother so much – he used to play too rough. I still had another brother and a sister to chase around.

A lady stranger came the next evening. She sat on the floor next to where I was batting around a crinkly little ball with my sister. Curious, I climbed into the lady's lap. She sat very still. I sniffed her and thought she smelled good – kind of kitchen-y, a nice, faint food smell. I didn't smell another cat or animal, like a dog. I don't much care for dogs. She gave me a gentle scratch around my ears and under my chin. Mmm, it felt so good I couldn't help purring. She talked to me in a soft, low voice meant for me alone. We were definitely having a moment.

Just then, my sister spoiled the mood by trying to climb into the lady's lap next to me. I did the first thing that came to mind: I kicked sister on the head with my hind foot. That's what I used to do when she tried to push me aside while I was nursing on our mother. Find your own lap to sit on! Sister tumbled backwards and slid to the floor. She lost interest in what I was doing and went back to playing with the crinkly little ball that wobbled all over the place when pounced on.

The nice lady picked me up so gently and put me on the floor. Why did she do that? Was she mad at me for kicking Sister? Now she picked up my brother. Really? She wanted to hold him, not me? Didn't she know I had chosen her? She stood up and carried him around the room on her shoulder. That had to stop! Again, I did the first thing that came to mind – I threw myself down in front of the lady's feet. The plan, if you could call it that, was to trip her so she would drop my brother and pick me up to see if I had been hurt. Then I would purr in her ear and she would never put me down. I had to try this again and again, because she didn't trip and didn't drop my brother, who was looking all too happy on her shoulder.

Then I heard her laugh, a nice sound people make. She put down my brother and picked me up. My plan had worked! Still laughing she snuggled me. Finally, I knew she had realized I had chosen her.

Putting me down next to my mother, she and my first lady talked and my new lady got out some of those little pieces of paper they value so much. Did that mean they knew I was valuable? I knew that already. Meanwhile my mother began carefully washing my face for the last time, all the while talking to me in silent cat language. She told me I was old enough to go to my own home. She had taught me all I needed to know to train my own person. She told me sometimes they wouldn't learn right away what I was trying to teach them, but to be patient and firm as I repeat the lesson. Remember, she emphasized, the cat is always right.

With that, my new and forever lady picked me up and put me in a box with bars in front. What? Was that any way to start a good relationship? She carried me in the box to her car. As she drove, I crouched in silence in the back of that box. I wanted to let her know that no fluffy blanket could make up for the fact that this was a cage!

At the new house the strangeness of it all was overwhelming. There was so much to see and smell. First my lady showed me where the litter box was. I obliged by climbing in and demonstrating my mastery of litter box etiquette. She approved. Next I was introduced to the food and water bowls, which I sampled to be polite. I was too excited to eat much. I could find my way back later by following my nose. Then I spotted a scratching post. Just the sight of it made my paws tingle. I squirmed down from her arms to work my claws on the scratching post, reaching up as high as I could. It felt so good! With a good scratching post available, I might be able to leave the sofa alone. I would check out the sofa later when I made a thorough examination of the house on my own.

Finally she lifted me into a cat bed. As cat beds go, it was okay, but I had no intention of spending much time there. I wanted to be with my lady. That started me thinking that I would need a better name for her. I wondered how she would feel if I thought of her as "Mommy?" I knew she was trying out names for me on the way home in the car. None of those names sounded right. I could only hope she wouldn't come up with something silly that I would be stuck with for the rest of my life.

I stayed in the cat bed for what I thought would be long enough so she wouldn't think I wasn't grateful, before hopping out and following the sounds of her getting ready for bed. It was time for her first lesson in "the cat is always right." I found her in her bed ready for sleep. To get up there on the bed I was going to have to climb. That comforter looked slippery. Good thing I had just sharpened my claws. I made a running start, landed partway up and clawed the rest of the way to the top. I heard a couple of little ripping sounds as I climbed. Just in case a few small tears might become an issue, I started purring. A lot of embarrassing little things can be smoothed over by being cute and loving.

Once on top of the bed I crept up next to my "Mommy." Yeah, Mommy it is. I like the sound of that. I curled up close where I could hear her heartbeat, just as I used to do with my cat mother. My new Mommy whispered some welcoming words and circled her arms around me. As we fell asleep my last thought was *My mother was right; I can do this.*

Ellen is proud to be a fourth generation Californian. After graduating with a Bachelor of Arts degree from San Francisco State she married, lived and worked in the San Francisco Bay Area. Now retired, she lives with her husband, Ford, in Pollock Pines, CA. She has written and published historical articles in such periodicals as *Sierra Heritage*, the *Overland Journal* and *Around Here Magazine*. In 2015, her history of early El Dorado County, *A Lovely And Comfortable Heritage Lost*, was published and is available for sale. As a member of the Placerville Shakespeare Club, Ellen helped research and write the well-received original presentation "El Dorado's True Gold Notable Women's Stories" in 2013.

Ellen is a member of the El Dorado Writer's Guild and Northern California Publishers & Authors group.

CLARITY ON A SUNDAY

KIMBERLY A. EDWARDS

The beach community of Kovalam on the southern tip of India fell under a mist of incense and cooking smoke as we ascended the slope on our way out of town. A driver named J.R. was transporting me, along with a British woman named Nancy, to the one cultural ritual that remained on my list: the elephant festival.

My boyfriend Frank was not happy with my decision to travel to an unknown temple several towns away. "Getting close to a bunch of elephants could be dangerous," he said that morning over a breakfast of eggs and buttered *naan* bread in the rooftop restaurant of our Best Western hotel.

"I can't know India if I don't experience an elephant festival," I said. Frank and I had traveled the world together, but this was the first time I was venturing out on my own. Maybe he was upset that I was leaving him alone for an afternoon.

"You never know what could happen," he warned. "Besides, you could learn just as much in a book."

Frank was mistaken; I was annoyed. There was nothing unsafe about an elephant festival. I'd seen the pageantry, the color, the praise heaped on them in newspapers and travel brochures. Only once in our five weeks in India had I heard about a villager getting trampled. But that was in a village up North. I was not going to let Frank's admonition keep me from an honored custom in the Southern India we loved.

Once over the slope, the terrain leveled out. Streets were impeccably clean, no clutter in sight. We passed village after village. A few goats ran loose. Not a discarded plastic bag in sight. Mothers, fathers, children, and grandparents moseyed along the shoulder of the road. There was impeccable order here in the South, everything calm and predictable. Why give elephants a bad rap?

"How far away is the temple?" I asked J.R. He turned to hear me in the backseat, flashing the side of his wire frame glasses. His skin was an even darkness, the color of coal after a flame lowers. He seemed American in spite of a heavy Indian accent. His driving was slow and steady, qualities I appreciate in a taxi driver, especially in India.

"Just down the road," he said. His voice rang softly, perhaps as gentle as the local people and elephants.

"Can't wait," I said. "We Americans like to see things first-hand, you know."

"We Brits, too" said Nancy, tightening the string of her hiking hat similar to mine. This was all I knew about her, except that she was a guest at the hotel in which Frank and I were staying.

It was exciting to think of what awaited. The majestic elephant wields a special place in Indian history. I had seen them sketched on tapestries, transporting royalty over the centuries. Some were kept almost as pets. They entertained princes, sashayed in velvet capes at religious celebrations and led Rajput warriors to victory. Prestige carried no symbol greater than the mighty elephant in a land of honor and tradition.

Nancy and I exchanged small talk for two hours until J.R. applied the brakes. He turned down a dirt road. The car bounced and wound through rising dust before coming to a stop.

"Here is where you get out," he said. "Go on ahead. Just enjoy yourselves, stay safe. I'll find you after it's over."

"Always," I said, putting on my hat. I kept the string loose.

A blaring sound system led the way. The dirt was tightly packed from the feet that came before us. Curry and incense scented the air. A crowd pressed against a wooden fence bordering a circus ring.

From a tall building across the ring emerged the elephants.

155

Each debuted with great celebrity: long introduction on an unseen mic, elevated pitch, murmurs and body shifts of onlookers. The revered lumbered around the ring to rousing approval as the announcer's voice grew impassioned. There was no need to understand the language because the people's actions said it all.

Nancy and I inched into the spectators, made up largely of men and some children. A dot of beige paint decorated the center of their foreheads. Next to the ring, shirtless young males in short white *sarongs* tied at their waist played drums and cymbals, while another group seemed slated for religious induction.

On the far side of the temple, a group of elephants awaited. Between their feet, handlers lounged. They chatted and exhaled cigarette smoke through massive gray pillars and fly-swatting tails.

As the sun beat down and the crowd swelled, more elephants joined those on the other side of the temple. Nancy and I navigated the assembly to get closer. Twenty elephants awaited the next phase of the program. As the afternoon wore on, they were mounted by young devotees, adorning the giants with tinseled silk parasols and swaying peacock plumes.

Not far in the distance, a bridge arched over a narrow street. Atop the bridge, people in floppy hats milled.

"Look at those tourists up there," I said to Nancy.

"Someone's bringing out chairs," she said.

"Oh, my God," I said. "They must be American." I remembered the quote from Paul Theroux: "Tourists don't know where they've been, travelers don't know where they're going."

"Maybe they get a better view up there," said Nancy.

"Afraid they'll get dirty getting too close," I scoffed. "You wouldn't find me up there. Yet they'll go home and brag that they saw it all, won't they?"

Nancy shook her head.

"Culture kept at a distance," I said. "Why bother coming to India?"

Nancy tightened the hat string at her neck.

"Arrogant, watching as if in a theatre. Next they'll be serving popcorn."

By now the handlers who were relaxing under the elephants were standing, patting the gray hides, herding them toward the thin road under the arch.

"Let's follow," I said.

"Everyone's headed down the grade, under the arched bridge," said Nancy.

"A parade!" I cheered.

We followed the locals, walking, skipping, limping down the street, passing under the arch where the tourists sat. As we exited the other side, the Sunday view of village leisure burst into view: families spread out on grass, three or four generations reclined on blankets, laughing, jostling, munching on treats. We waved at kids as we strolled. They waved back. We traded peace signs. This was India close-up. There was nothing more affirming than smiles and welcomes.

Over a loudspeaker came a voice, ardent in tone and pitch, which we interpreted as a signal to get ready for the procession. We speeded our pace to join the locals lining the street, finding a spot in front of a stone building. Meanwhile, the tour group watched from the bridge, their necks cranked forward, faces masked by binoculars.

More people joined us along the street. A drum roll began. Everyone looked down the road for the elephants. The announcer let out a torrent that likely was a prayer.

The star attractions began to appear. They trudged in single file, a boy atop each, attended by an entourage carrying sticks. At a pivotal point, the escorts prodded the elephants to stop. A voice cried into the loudspeaker. Hands thrusted into the elephants' mouths a stalk of bananas, quickly consumed, inciting applause.

"Can't get much safer than this," I said to Nancy. I unzipped my purse to take out my camera, but decided this experience was much too unique to capture in photos.

Just as I zipped my purse closed, a scream arose in the

157

direction of the elephants parading this way. The alarm came like a cannonball, source unknown, but the effect set off vocal explosions, echoing urgency. It was impossible to see what was happening because of a curve in the road. In the maze I saw bodies scrambling, engulfing the surroundings into a swirling vortex. There was no time to wonder what to do. Instinctively I grabbed the belt of the local youth next to me and ran with him towards the stone building behind us.

Stampeding feet came behind. Then more. And more. My back pressed against the stone building. As the distressed leaned in, every one of my senses faded: no microphone voice, screams, dust, heat, scent of bananas or incense.

Terror took over me as I understood that the setback of buildings from an Indian village street meant no cushion against a surging mass. I was stuck, pinned to the building, in danger of being crushed. Regret clasped me and held me. I had three kids. A grandchild on the way. Would Frank know where I was? Would he ever find me? Why did he let me come? Time slowed. I remembered every warning he had ever given me.

I was still breathing when the pressure abated. Slowly the crowd moved back toward the street, releasing me from uneven stone.

For the next several minutes, I wandered in a daze. I found Nancy. Neither of us spoke as we hugged, knowing we would forever be cemented in each other's memory. Feet away lay my hat, trodden but intact.

J.R. came sprinting. "Let's get back in the car."

"An elephant—out of control," I said, barely able to utter the words.

"*Nahi,*" he said.

"Everyone just started running," said Nancy.

"It wasn't the elephants who acted up," said J.R. "Most likely an elephant took a step to the side and the people panicked. The elephants always get the blame."

"Mob mentality," said Nancy.

J.R. nodded. "Last year a man was killed at this temple when someone screamed."

"What?" cried Nancy. We looked at each other. No one had told us that our own kind could get us trampled to death.

"Not from an elephant," said JR. "The crowd."

"I've seen enough," I said, jumping into the car. I slid down in my seat.

During the drive back to Kovalam, Nancy and I stayed quiet except to agree that one elephant festival was enough in a lifetime.

As my mind unwound, I debated about recounting this experience to Frank. My eagerness to get close had almost gotten me in trouble. Would it be better to not tell him? But wait, his warning had been misdirected, as he anticipated problems with the wrong mammals.

By the time we came to the slope marking the descent into Kovalam, the ocean emerged from under the incense and cooking smoke. Sparkling blue waters extended as far as the eye could see. That's when I realized that distinctions in life may not be as clear as we think. Where they start is not always where they end. People to animals. Annoyance to love. Tradition to universality. I didn't need to go to India to experience how scared people act. And boy, was I glad to see Frank.

 Kimberly A. Edwards, president of the California Writers Club Sacramento, writes articles, memoir, and personal essays. She has championed writers for 30+ years. In addition to having founded a monthly newsletter for writers, she has written for Writer's Digest and other publications serving women, teens, travelers, seniors, and general audiences. Each summer she attends the Kenyon

Review Writer's Workshop (literary nonfiction). She is an alumnus of Squaw Valley Community of Writers (fiction). Kim likes helping fellow writers turn memories into enduring stories in the Renaissance Society Memories and Memoir Seminar. She has been a featured reader at Writers on Air. Currently she is at work on a History Press Book on early Sacramento motorcycling. A member of the American Society of Journalists and Authors and the Independent Book Publishers Association, she likes nothing better than encouraging writers to pursue their dream and urges them to never give up.

Contact Kim at Kimberlyedwards00@comcast.net.

A DOG WITH A BLOG

NANCY J. MILLER

A boy jumps out of his car and dashes towards us as we take a walk through familiar sights and scents. He asks my Person what kind of dog I am. "I'm a dog," I want to say, "blonde and handsome or he wouldn't be asking." My Person hands him my business card and tells him to check out my blog. A blog! What kind of dog has a blog? I must be a blog dog, although my Person tells the boy I am a Pepper.

My Person tells me that I am getting all of the attention—so true—so she started a blog for me to record all the sights and smells she notices walking with a dog (me!). I know she started the blog to get attention for her coaching and writing business even though she says it's all about me. I happen to like her quite a lot, but I don't see people oohing and aahing over her.

After a walk, my Person says she needs to write in my blog. As she reads it to me, she doesn't notice that I am taking a short nap.

> Pepper looks up in a tree to see a squirrel,
> The squirrel growls at the little dog who doesn't seem to notice,
> Nose to the ground, Pepper is off on his next adventure.

My Person has a name, but I just think of her as my Person. I adopted her after living at her house for a few months—not really sure about time—it happened very gradually. I was very anxious and a little depressed when I first met the people who took me home. The man, as I called him, said, "No! We are not taking HIM home." HIM being me, I assume, and home being his house. Everything was a blur after that. There was

161

some petting—them petting me—not the other way around. Then I was hugged, which felt good, and I was taken to their house. My Person told the man that I have a Pepper Personality. I'm sure she made that up. She said I could sit at her feet for hours, or at a moment's notice jump up, and be ready to go outside for a walk. She told the man he would get used to me.

I have been in many houses. Some were better than others. I remember a house that was warm and cozy with my own blanket and lots of love and hugs. But the last one was very bad. I was kept in a cold room they called a garage with food and water. I let them know I didn't like it. I was very noisy. How could they miss that? The man with the long legs talked very loud and said I was a bad dog. I understood him. Why didn't he understand me? I just wanted a warm bed and an occasional hug.

One morning I had a great idea. I knew I was faster than the man with the long legs and loud voice, so I dashed in the house so fast he didn't even see me. I ran through the house looking for a corner where I could hide, when the loud man came after me with a long hard thing. He hit me over the head with it. I ran back out to the cold place and found a box to hide behind. The next time I ran for the door, the man kicked me and it really hurt. The next thing I remember is being at the place with lots of other dogs. I was shivering and shaking in a cage.

Lots of people walked by and looked at me. Then they looked at the cage and said I had anxiety. Not good. They would shake their heads and walk away. That is when my Person came and said I needed her. She said she helps people who are stressed, and maybe she could help me. I think she really just needed me.

When I got to my new house, my Person gave me hugs and treats. She knows how to make friends. She reminded me of the person with the warm house and blanket. When my Person's man came toward me, I shook all over and peed on his leg. Wow! Was he mad! I'm not sure what happened there.

I knew what a loud voice meant, and I ran fast! Okay. I peed on him a few times, and he forgave me.

My Person said she wouldn't be gone long but it seemed like forever. I don't like to be left alone. My Person used to put treats all around the house. It was so fun to find them behind and under things. It didn't take long to find all the treats and then I was afraid. When my Person got home I felt better and ran around the house, chowing down on all the treats I had found earlier.

The next time she left, I heard her voice on a hard round thing. I took a big sniff. It wasn't her. More barking. I found something else that smelled like her, but it wasn't. More barking. Then before she left, she put something around my neck. I barked and—psst—something sprayed in front of my face. I didn't like it, but I barked anyway.

When I was left alone, I didn't know what to do with myself. Sometimes I ran and barked, chewed on the walls, and made a mess. Oops! Then, I spent some time in a small room with something blocking the way out. I made a big mess. Couldn't help myself. I just get so excited. I heard my Person say she wrote about my anxiety on my blog. Not what I would have told about myself. She said her friends sent pictures and stories about their dogs for my blog. One dog eats socks. Yuck! I prefer chicken. My Person gave me lots of love and hugs, and I sniffed smells in front of my nose. She said it would help me stay home alone. It didn't work.

I spent some time in an outside place with a big wall around it. Maybe I could find my Person if I could only get out. I dug and dug. I'm good at digging. I finally got under the wall. I started running. I ran until I needed to sit. Someone scooped me up and put me back behind the wall. Not this again. I started to dig. Then I heard my Person. Soon I was back inside with my blanket and my Person. Maybe she would keep me after all. Or, maybe not. I soon found myself in a cage again. My Person showed me a big soft cage. I knew cages; I had been in one a few times. This one wouldn't hold me. When my Person left, I found a way out. I was free, but only briefly.

Then came a box I couldn't open. When my Person started moving faster and making familiar sounds, I knew it was time to find a dark corner. If there was one thing worse than being left alone, it was being alone in the box. I heard people say I am part cockapoo, and I might be getting just a little bit round in places where my favorite treats go, but I can squeeze in to very tight spaces when I get scared. Maybe I get smaller. I hear my Person make a lot of uhs and ughs as she looks for me under and around things. Then somehow she always gets me out and puts me in the box. Then she leaves. I am alone. I shake and whine to let them know to come back. No one hears. I just scratch and scratch at the box trying to get out. My paws hurt. No one comes. I am afraid I will go back again to the place with all the dogs. No one will want me. I dig harder.

I guess they weren't my people after all. I heard them both agree to send me to a doggie boot camp that the dog doctor recommended. I am at that place. It looked like a house, the place they took me, but now I am in a very small cage. There are other dogs around. Sometimes I can run around but it's really no fun. Then I'm on what they call a leash. They tell me what to do and pull on the leash. I don't like it so I just sit there. They pull and use very loud words. I sit. This goes on for a while. One day I hear a voice say my people want me back. My people want me back! I'm going home. I heard my Person say she wrote something about the terrible place with the small cage on my blog—she thinks she knows what I am thinking and what was happening—which is okay. She is a writer after all, so she is allowed to write about my thoughts and happenings even if she makes up some of it. Most is actually true.

Next came the bag that moved with my people. Yes. My people. I adopted them; even the man. He carried me in the bag that moved. We went in the car, to busy places, or just walking around. It was a happy time. One day I was in a busy place with my Person and some others. They said we were going to a bridal shop with dresses. I was in my bag sitting, and I got to stick my head out and get a nice rub on the head. I like a nice rub or pat on the head when they ask first. Even sitting still, I don't get scared in my bag that moves. I know I will move with it.

One day a black fluffy dog showed up to live with us. I wasn't alone anymore. They said her name was Sally. My Person wrote in my blog that we walk together side by side and people smile and say, "hi," as they pass by. She even wrote a poem about us. Sally liked to take the lead when we went for walks even though I could tell she didn't know where she was going. She didn't know her place as second dog, but I liked the walks so I didn't bite her. We went to the sandy place and ran in the water. I know water. I just didn't know it could be so fun! I look up and feel the breeze across my nose and I'm happy to have a home, my people, and a pal.

I heard my Person say that she had to close my blog because the man at the doggie boot camp was really mad when he read what she wrote about me being there. She probably wrote how I felt about it even though she only saw how sick and scared I was when I got home. So, I am happy that she writes about my thoughts and feelings even though I am just a dog. Now I have my people, and I am a happy dog without a blog.

Nancy J. Miller, M.S. is a Career Counselor/Certified Life Coach at Creative LifeWork Design in Elk Grove, CA. She is author of the books, *Fire Up Your Profile For LifeWork Success* and *Vegetable Kids in the Garden* to promote healthy relationships, lifestyles and self-esteem. Nancy publishes professional articles on careers, business and health. She gives presentations on the Vegetable Personality Styles™ she developed based on the four basic vegetable colors and the way they grow. She enjoys reading and dancing with her grandchildren, and she has fond memories of walks on California beaches with her cocker spaniel, Pepper.

Contact Nancy at success@nancyjmiller.solutions, visit her website www.tealpublishing.com, like her Vegetable Kids in the Garden Facebook page.

SACRAMENTO CITY KITTY COMMITTEE

JAN HAAG

I't's a Saturday afternoon like countless others where I've found myself walking outside the old portable building at Sacramento City College where I taught journalism for 20 years. Though the department has moved across campus to a new building, I still come to the portable on weekends and holidays to do a bit of public service.

I step through the bushes next to the building where I've installed a plastic bin, turned on its side, that holds three plastic dishes: one for dry food, one for wet food and one for water. I look for the gray feral kitty who is the primary eater—I hope. Every year I worry that Haroshea won't make it through another winter. Cold weather is tough on ferals, which is why I give her wet food to give her something more substantial. Of course, I have no way of knowing which cats (or other critters, for that matter) eat here. But I hope Haroshea is one of them. She was born under the building years ago, and even after I moved across campus, I felt a duty to continue her care.

Since the move, Haroshea has weekday feeders—currently Doug and Yuriko, physics professors who teach in the building. Before them, Alena, a custodian, fed Haroshea on weekdays. A host of other volunteers have pitched in over the years, and other college employee volunteers like me feed cats across campus.

I always look for her behind the building, calling "kitty, kitty!" Lately I have not seen her. I often holler to no one in particular, "Food, baby!" and, finishing my task, return to my car, shaking my head about this responsibility I took on long ago.

* * *

It started more than twenty years ago with a dead cat under the trailer. For days I could smell something foul wafting through the thin metal walls and coming up under the floorboards as I advised the student journalists of the *Express* newspaper, or lectured about commas and thesis statements to English students, or refereed creative writing students haggling over pieces for the literary journal.

I called the campus maintenance people, asking them to check. "We can't find anything," they told me. I called again. "Really smelly," I said, raising my voice a bit. "Smells like something died under there." The voice on the other end promised to dispatch someone to look. I got a call: "Still nothing," someone said.

I've been taking care of animals all my adult life, and, unfortunately, I know dead ones when I smell them. One weekend day I donned some crummy clothes and crawled under the trailer, toward the smell. And sure enough, almost in the center, there was a none-too-pretty former black cat, on its side, mouth open. I had a stick and scooped its remains into a bag I'd brought with me and crawled out from under the building, realizing, as I did so, that this cat was likely feral and had made its home under us for who knew how long?

I resisted the urge to deposit the bag on the desk of the people who'd insisted there was nothing dead under the trailer. But (after properly disposing of the poor creature) instead I began putting out dry food and water for cats on the porch at night. In winter I put out wet food. I rarely saw the cats, but they clearly made appearances. The food disappeared. I'd occasionally scare one that was eating outside my office door or see one streaking across the parking lot toward the football stadium.

Once in a while a cat would show up and just sit outside my office door. Maybe cry a little. That always meant trouble. Feral cats don't generally cry at people for food; tame ones, imitating kittens do. A crying cat had likely been dumped and needed a home. They don't do well among the ferals, who are, after all, wild animals. And so, one after another, I'd scoop up the dumped kitties, take them to the vet to check them out and find them homes—often that home was mine. I haven't adopted a cat from a proper agency in more than 20 years, though I've found good homes for a number of great cats who appeared at the portable. As I often tell people, "I keep the broken ones."

One day my life changed forever when I got an email from Holly Kivlin, a woman who worked across campus. "I hear you're feeding cats out by the stadium," she wrote to me. "I'm feeding ferals near the cafeteria. We should talk."

That was, as Bogart said in *Casablanca*, the beginning of a beautiful friendship.

Holly, it turned out, was doing a lot more than just feeding cats. She was also trapping them and taking them to be spayed or neutered. She had them tested for feline leukemia, and if they were positive, she had them euthanized. All on her own dime. She returned the healthy ferals to the campus to hold the space and prevent others from showing up.

I'd had a few ferals fixed, as we used to say, but mostly I was just a feeder. Holly (who is one of the kindest souls on the planet) immediately volunteered to help me trap and transport cats to a nearby veterinarian who'd spay and neuter at cost.

Holly and her husband Joel met me at nights and on weekends and taught me to set traps (canned mackerel is the best bait to lure a cat into a trap, I learned), pick up the trap with cat inside, take it to the vet, bring it home for at least one overnight and return it to campus. When I'd see a new cat in the area, I'd call her across campus. "Come on over," she'd say. "I have a trap under my desk." I'd go borrow a trap, setting it at night and waiting inside my office to hear the open door snap shut, then go out and try to calm the poor freaked-out cat inside.

The college had had a problem with feral cats since it opened its doors on Freeport Boulevard in 1926. I'm sure others did their best to cope with the cats. But it was Holly who organized people across campus to help and who dubbed us the Sacramento City Kitty Committee. She named each cat and kept track of its vet visits and treatments. She'd put up displays on campus with photos of the cats, and people donated food and money for the cause. So many people on campus, from the president to custodians, were sympathetic and helped in ways we couldn't have anticipated.

Some would call if they heard or saw cats crying. Others helped us pull feral kittens out of hiding places and trap their mamas, fostering them and trying to keep the families together until the kittens were old enough to be tamed, fixed and placed in homes. One year we trapped and removed 38 cats from campus.

One pregnant mama gave birth in my back bedroom, then vamoosed out a partially open door. I never saw her again, but my partner Dick and I took turns bottle feeding the kittens day in and day out every three hours. I even brought the kittens to school in a cat carrier, and my students helped with feedings. Those babies were so used to being handled, they grew up to be two of the sweetest cats I've ever known.

When Holly retired a few years ago, about the time I moved from the trailer, we lost the heart and soul of the Sacramento City Kitty Committee—though she and Joel, who live nearby, still come to campus on weekends to help with feeding when the regular feeders are not there. The work of the committee continues, but it's not the same without Holly.

As for me, I keep saying that my cat feeding days will end when I know that Haroshea is no longer with us. Now and then I get a call from someone on campus who's seen a sick or dying cat. One of my favorite cats was found near death on a heating exhaust grate outside. The IT guys brought the kitty inside where it died, and then they buried the kitty out behind the baseball field. I cried when I learned that.

There are so many big-hearted people on my campus, and it does my heart good when I hear stories like this. It seems a small thing to do for ones in need in our community—not unlike the weekly campus food distributions or seasonal coat and professional clothing giveaways. Small kindnesses go a long way, I believe, and, working for so long at an educational institution, I like to think that City College not only teaches people what they need to know to go on to other colleges and jobs, but also has a generous soul that embraces everyone— human and critter.

So it is that I do my rounds on weekends and leave food in more than one spot for Haroshea and others who might need it around the trailer. I hope she's dry and safe and warm in winters. I hope she finds cool spots with the food and water we leave in summers. I hope, to paraphrase Mother Teresa, that this small thing we do with great love makes a tiny difference in the world.

Jan Haag teaches journalism and creative writing at Sacramento City College. She is the chair of the journalism department, where she co-founded the student literary journal and currently advises the campus newspaper and journalistic magazine. Jan is the author of a book of poems, *Companion Spirit*, published by Amherst Writers & Artists Press. She leads weekly creative writing workshops in Sacramento, has written two novels and had work published in many journals and anthologies. She is also the co-publisher of River Rock Books in Sacramento. Her website is www.janishaag.com.

IGUANA

MATTHIAS MENDEZONA

While in my early teens and living with my grandfather, I hunted every day. I had a routine. I was in the mountains by 5:30 am, usually with a gofer to pick up the game. By 6 am I would be in a spot where the wild doves would feed. I sat down with my .22 rifle and waited. Soon they would come in twos, threes and sometimes in a heart-pounding group of five or more. I would take careful aim and shoot one.

This pattern repeated itself until about 7 am when the birds, their breasts filled to bursting with food, flew down to the mangrove area to sleep off the heat of the day.

I would pick up my gear and trudge to the *Pis-an* pond, a *Subano*[1] name for the creek it originally was before my grandfather dammed it up. Approaching the *Pis-an* was cautious business. Well before I was within eyeshot of the water, I treaded lightly and moved in slow motion because I was already being watched.

The iguana lived there. They were called *Ibid* by the locals. From the trees and half submerged stumps in the shadows the Ibid watched. I learned not to jerk my body when the water splashed as one iguana, and then another, abandoned their perches for the safety underwater where they could stay submerged interminably. Many times other iguana opted to stay where they were, confident that their skin color had adapted to their surroundings well enough to make detection impossible.

Because there was no way to know how many iguana the

---

[1] Mountain people who live scattered throughout the hinterlands mostly of the Zamboanga Peninsula in the island of Mindanao, Philippines. The first part of their name, "Suba", means river.

pond had, I would continue walking to the levee. I would find a shadow and slowly sit down, there to stay immobile for well over an hour. Only my eyes would move, scanning the banks, the trees and the stumps, especially those at the far end of the pond where the foliage was thick, the branches extending over the water.

If I got lucky, an iguana would relax and begin to move, ever so slowly. That variation in the landscape sometimes caught my eye. I would raise my .22 carefully and shoot for the shoulder or the head. The iguana had to be killed with that one shot because this was the only sure way to retrieve him from the ground or the water. A wounded iguana was almost certainly a loss, diving into the water and disappearing until it either died or surfaced unseen at some far corner of the pond. Bagging an iguana meant good eating, as they were as tender and tasty as chicken. It also meant that one was patient and skillful.

* * *

The other day I was ripped off in my California home. My wife and I had been working in the garage and left the garage door open while we chatted with a visitor in the kitchen. Within a forty-five minute window, someone walked deep into the garage and rolled out my multi-layered toolbox on wheels. When my wife and I resumed our garage work, we soon discovered the toolbox missing.

The thief left intact everything else in the garage. He only wanted that one thing and went for it. This was 4:00 in the afternoon. How did he pull it off in plain sight? We live at the throat of a cul-de-sac. This guy has *cojones*, I thought. Unless of course *he also lives in the cul-de-sac himself.*

I walked directly to my neighbor *A* at the end of the cul-de-sac. He did not have a steady job. His garage was chock full of equipment, tools, spare parts and assorted odds and ends, requiring him to park his vehicles outside. He was constantly working on car or motorcycle engines, oftentimes at 2:30 in the

173

morning. Men pulled in and out of his driveway at all hours, transacting with him in deals of unknown content. One such man saw me approaching and pointed uneasily to A, who was soldering an electronic component on a motorcycle.

"Hey, A, I just wanted to tell you that I got ripped off just now," I said.

"Oh, yeah?" A retorted. No surprise. No shock registering.

"Yeah. Someone walked into my garage and wheeled out my toolbox."

"Oh," A said.

"I just wanted to let you know. Heads up, man," I said and walked away. Something was wrong with that scene.

I talked to my neighbor Henry, an eighteen-year original homeowner in the area. Henry, a steelworker, told me that he too had left his garage door open and unattended several months previously. In that window of time, someone stole his grass cutter from the wall on one side of his parked truck. The same person then went to the other side of Henry's truck, picked up his toolbelt with tools and his oxy-acetylene welding set, then left everything else untouched.

"Sounds like the same Modus as my case, Henry," I told him.

"Yup, and I know who did it too," Henry replied.

"Who?" I asked.

"It's that A down the street. He's on crank, he's up at all the strangest hours, and he's got all kinds of people pulling in and out of his house with all sorts of deals. It's him," Henry said.

Henry gave me the rundown of who the original neighborhood homeowners were and how they had no trouble before A came along several years ago. Henry and I traded phone numbers.

"Here's one iguana that needs watching." I thought of the iguana that I had hunted as a teen.

The iguana had been watching me long before I became aware of it. I would wait at my *Pis-an* pond and observe. I learned patience a long time ago. Sooner or later the iguana would move. I was in no hurry.

Matthias Mendezona is Jesuit educated from Grade School through College and obtained a University of the Philippines Master's degree in Business Management. A current faculty member of the University of Phoenix CA campus, he has authored three books that can be ordered from Amazon either in hard copy or Kindle, *You Can't Save 80 Million Filipinos! But You Can Build Me a Park.*, *How Sweet the Mango, No?* and a prize-winning poetry collection awarded by Northern California Publishers & Authors entitled *Rumination.* He lives with his wife Mikey in Sacramento, CA within driving distance from three of his four daughters, sons-in-law, grandchildren, and the outdoors that they frequent.

His website is www.amazon.com/matthiasmendezona.

REGARDING CRICKET

M.L. HAMILTON

L ast March, my beautiful Golden girl didn't jump off the bed with her usual energy. She just stood, hanging her head. I thought it was arthritis. I was wrong.

Many vet visits, many tests, many scans later, and we were told the horrible truth: she had splenetic cancer and we had at most two weeks left with her. At first I couldn't get my head around it. I still can't. I think of her every morning when I wake up. She's the last thing on my mind when I go to sleep. I miss her. I suppose I always will.

All dogs are amazing. All dogs bring things to our lives that make it richer, better, more bearable. My current dogs (Bailey and Comet) are the reason I get up in the morning. They're the reason I can't wait to get home at night. I adore them.

But there are some dogs who enter our life that just fit. They seamlessly weave themselves into the fabric of who we are and become irreplaceable. Cricket was that for me.

Now it would be very easy for this story to become a gut-wrenching, cathartic explanation of the depth of loss I feel without her, but I don't want that. True, the end of her life was scarring, but the living of her life was magnificent, joyful...beautiful. I want to concentrate on that. I want to tell you a story of the Cricket I knew. The Cricket who approached life as if every room, every park, every arena was hers and her job was to welcome you and make you feel happiness.

So, in honor of a dog who truly was the hostess with the mostest, here's Cricket's Agility Fail.

* * *

I truly adore my Golden Retriever. If ever there was an angel on earth, such a divine being must inhabit that dog's body. She is everything a dog should be: loyal, gentle, giving...but she is not agility material.

Years ago, my friend Karen and I decided we would take our two dogs to obedience school. It was fun and we learned something. I'm a great believer that if you come away from any experience a little smarter, it was worth the effort. Once it ended, I missed it. It was an opportunity to be with other dog lovers and a regular time where Karen and I could get together and catch up. Cricket did reasonably well. In fact, her affable personality won most of the people over and I came away proud of myself for having such a well-mannered dog. I got greedy.

Looking for something else that Karen and I could do with our dogs, I stumbled upon agility. I've seen it on television many times. Brilliant teams of dogs and handlers racing around a course, weaving intricate patterns and finishing with hugs and doggy kisses. It seemed like the perfect thing and I was certain Cricket would be a natural. As is human nature, I ignored the fact that all the dogs I saw on television were of three varieties: Australian Shepherds, Border Collies or Shelties. I believe in equal rights, so I told myself there was no law that said a Golden Retriever couldn't be a Grand Master.

Well, they can't. I'm convinced of this. Cricket is a disaster. Worse still, she is comic relief.

Karen and I have a good-natured rivalry about our dogs. It was present in obedience and it's present now. We each want our dogs to be the star, to outshine the other just that little amount. We tease each other about cheating and practicing behind the other's back. But now it just isn't fair. We both know who is master here.

Chance looks like an agility dog. He bounces between the weave poles with vigor and purpose. He tears through the tunnel and comes out, ready to take the next obstacle. And when he slams into that tire and sends it dancing on its chains, you feel the power in the pit of your stomach. He is out there to compete. He is out there to win. And each time he strings together the ridiculously complicated tasks, Karen turns to me and smirks.

Imagine Lance Armstrong racing a toddler on a tricycle. That is Cricket and I. Cricket takes the weave poles as if she's afraid she might chip her manicure. When she makes it to the other side, she pauses to look around and see if everyone is adoring her flowing golden coat. When she goes through the tunnel, she pops out and waits for someone to bring her her reward.

And then there are the times when she just...she just...well, loses it. During one incident, we were supposed to take the weave poles, cross behind the dogs, and send them into the tunnel. I watched everyone else go and I knew it wasn't going to happen. Of course, Chance aced the entire sequence and came out of the tunnel fully prepared to do whatever else they asked of him.

I could feel my shoulders droop. It was my turn. I managed to stuff her into the weave poles, then walked along beside her as she meandered through. I could already tell her mind wasn't on this. She had her head up and was looking both ways, scoping out her adoring public. She came out of the weave and I motioned her to the tunnel, crossing around behind her.

I had seen everyone else hit that obstacle and go through it. Not Cricket. She breezed right on by. In frustration, I turned to look at the instructor, hoping for some pearl of wisdom, or at least commiseration. The trainer wasn't looking at me. Her eyes went beyond me outside the arena. In a calm as you please voice, she said, "Cricket has left the building."

I whipped back around and saw my son racing after Cricket. She was going up and down the line of waiting dogs, wagging her tail and kissing them on the muzzles. I swear I could just hear her saying, "Hi, dog, welcome to my arena. How are you, dog?"

My son and I talked with her sternly after that and jerry-rigged some obstacles in the backyard to practice upon, but I had little confidence in their success. We also took her to the dog park and practiced some jumps with her, hoping to get an edge on the competition.

Her next escapade was epic. Once again, we were supposed to go through multiple obstacles. This time she was supposed to do a jump, then go into the tunnel. As always, I positioned myself at the back of the line, feeling that familiar sinking in my stomach.

Chance was perfect, reminding me of the quarterback of the football team, confident and secure in his superiority. Then came Cricket. We made the jump and surprisingly, we went into the tunnel. From there it was mayhem.

She blazed out of the tunnel and zipped past me. She took off running around the perimeter of the arena, going full tilt, her butt tucked down and her head thrown back, ears flapping in the wind. Once again my son chased after her, but there was no stopping this madness. Another spin around the arena, dust flying from beneath her paws, over a jump, and then inexplicably, back into the tunnel for a second go-round.

Not even the instructors could help me. Everyone was standing in an amazed cluster, laughing so hard it was a miracle they remained standing. After a third pass around the arena, she came to us, panting and smiling as if she had stolen the show, which she had. As she and I moved back to our spot at the end of the line, Karen looked over at me, tears of laughter in her eyes, and said, "She seems so flighty."

Seems? Ain't no seems about it.

Odds are she and I will not be advancing at the end of this class. Her crazy antics have most likely sealed our fate, but I can't be too upset about it. She is so darn happy with her failure that I have to be happy about it too. It is so much more important to greet every dog coming into the arena and act like the prom queen garnering votes, or turn even the most dedicated handler into a mass of giggles.

Mostly I enjoy being with her and watching her prance her way around, as Karen puts it, "like Paris Hilton." She makes me laugh and for a while, I don't take myself so seriously. That's enough. So we'll never don an agility medal and we'll never have a Grand Master Championship, but there isn't a single other dog in that ring that fails with such panache.

So, here's to you, Angel Dog. I have a mental picture in my mind of you standing at the gates of Heaven, golden hair flowing, greeting all the dogs and people as they come up because of course, you've made Heaven your own and who else would they pick to greet everyone. And when I get there myself, I can't wait to tell you, "Hello, my beautiful friend."

M. L. Hamilton teaches high school English and journalism in Central California. She always dreamed of publishing her own novel.

That dream came true. Her first novel, *Emerald*, was published by Wild Wolf Publishing in 2010. In 2013, the *Peyton Brooks' Mysteries* were born, allowing her to branch into a new genre. After seven novels in that series, she moved the main character into the FBI.

In addition to teaching and writing, she has three sons, two dogs, and three cats. And sometimes a stray rabbit living under her deck.

LETTERS TO MY FIRST LOVES, IF HORSES COULD READ

DEBORAH MELTVEDT

Horse #1

I called you Toby after my first crush, the teenage boy who worked the Mobil gas station. I was only three or four, but I knew enough about love and beauty to name a horse after the cutest boy who offered inflated tires and security, as my mother pulled into the station.

But while Toby asked if he could "fill 'er up" my gaze went from his eyes to the sight of the flying horse emblem that gleamed in the night as my mother, my sisters and I sat waiting. Like that sign, you, too, were plastic and safe, the perfect try-out for me as my first ride, and I bounced you like crazy in our family room and hallways. With coiled rings and sloping seat, you became my introduction to joy.

Do you still hate me for giving you away?

It was my mother, you know. She was tired of you sitting in the corner, unused and unridden. I was getting too big for unreal things.

But I fought to keep you, you know? I even cried when we gave you to Lorena's kids and hated them climbing over you with sticky hands and wide-eyed looks. You were supposed to be mine. Always. Even with dust on your saddle, I wanted you to stay.

I named you Toby, not so much after the boy, but after the flying horse. He was cute, but you were the closest to launching me to the stars. And we gave you away.

Horse #2

I couldn't have you for real, so I drew you, all over my graph paper and math homework, on sidewalks and Mother's Day cards. I was good at ears and manes and great big butts, but lousy with the tips of mouths and that fourth hoof flying off the page. I apologize for making your nostrils too big or your tail too long.

But, even in ink, you gave me pride. Made me want to be better. Made me good at something. So when I couldn't show the world the right answer in algebra or geometry, I substituted you. Your copied beauty ended up on refrigerator doors, back to school night bulletin boards, and on the inside of high school locker walls.

You ended up memorized and sketched in the corners of a very stupid heart.

Horses #3 -11

More plastic. There were seven or eight of you. 99cents to twelve dollars. Spotted, bent-legged, one even saddled. I brought you down from the highest shelf when Jackie or Janet showed up on rainy days. In our bedrooms, you galloped over shag carpet and eight-year-olds' calves. You reared up in delight, our tiny hands cradling your back.

How did we not know we wouldn't own the real you? We had even given you names.

Horse #12

You never bit me, not once. Standing on tiptoe, just shy of thirteen, I held out sweetness. You took the carrot with those velvet lips, nibbled my shirt, butt-headed my backside, tossed your own head side to side with indignation, stared me down, but never once bit me.

When all the world had begun to pinch and the teeth of teachers and the mouths of fathers and the smiles of bad boys (you warned me about) flashed so wide I thought their lightning would burn me, you never broke skin. You didn't judge. You didn't bare anything at all but your silken back sloped slightly, as if you knew I needed a quiet place to lean.

Horse #13

I loved your big nose. And your mane and your flank and your big brown eyes I can still picture all these years later. I was just bike riding on a bored, Central Valley day and came upon you, a jolt of glory, and I dropped my bike in summer grass to meet you.

You leaned the biggest head over that old white fence, your nose seemed a million inches long, but it was as if God herself reached down and plucked wide open that smiling part inside of me that constantly needed prying. Almost as if fate said, "Look, here is a horse for you!" Not to own. Or ride. But you were there just to remember there is grandeur in the world. To make my heart smile.

And you did. You, with your tangled mane and charcoal coat, looked at me and the whole world spun and the whole world forgave me.

I still remember your eyes. Horse's eyes are the best irises ever. And you looked at me like you got me, like you knew I needed loving more than any other creature, human or not. This is when I knew the truest sense of love I have ever been given in minutes.

Do you remember nuzzling my neck? Head rubbing my side? I was only thirteen when I met you. You didn't care about my skin or face or frizzy hair. There you stood, swishing tail, waiting. Waiting for me to feed you dull yellow grass I pulled on the other side of the fence.

You were only mine for minutes.

But, in your eyes, you forgave better than Jesus.

And you let me pull your ears.

Horses #14 – 17

You were our saviors. As girls, we wanted wildness, tried to find it on our father's backs in swimming pools in July, when the sun was still wanted, when our legs were still small and dark and crossed against our Dad's sunburned chest and we shouted "Throw me! Throw me!" Then hands reached back and we flew into the deep end, laughing because we wanted flight, screaming because we needed wildness.

In fall, we settled for a swing set after school, pumping our legs fast, before our thighs were liabilities and we found ways to hate ourselves. Then, there you were! Free rides at the Fresno County Fair. That first spread across your pony back was better than bike riding, better than imagined flying. We didn't care the flight was slow as turtles, your mane like straw. On you, our grin was so alive!

Then came the tall ones, bigger than our Dad's shoulders. And we weren't even scared.

Our best friend's Grandfather's ranch, San Joaquin Valley heat, 105°, they cupped our sneakers and in trust we mounted you, the tall black one.

Our thighs, our tender thighs, before they shuddered in love, before they struggled into last year's jeans or this year's skirt, before hate, our thighs straddled you. And passion was truly born. Wildness whipped through fat and femur, through blood and bone, and we laughed together because we fell in love with you.

We screamed because it was one of the first times we girls truly loved ourselves.

Horse #18

Thank you for not jumping off the Andes mountain in Ecuador with me on your back when I know you were pissed off for hiking another American up the mountain so she could have a famous adventure in her thirties and write about it one day.

Thank you for being better than that.

Horse #19

I forgot your name, but they rented you to me on my honeymoon in Kauai for a three hour ride when I said I was a better rider than my new husband.

I knew from the start you were angry at Rick and his horse, Pekake, because he was mine and Pekake wasn't yours. At first you wouldn't go near the both of them, just kept them in sight, my husband's back and Pekake's backside, swaying in the wind. But you had your plan. You tricked me into thinking how romantic this was when you suddenly trotted up next to Rick and Pekake. For a brief moment, we were like Honeymooners in the movies: Two riders, two horses, riding together towards sunset.

And then you attacked her.

Even drew blood, but Rick stayed on Pekake, grabbing her mane, even though you and I both knew he was a lousy rider. And when we returned to the ranch, you heard the ranch boys welcome back Pekake saying "good horse!" and tipping their hat. But when you and I rode in, the boys all looked away, and one of them muttered something like "Satan". But you, unlike the rest of us, held your head high, and delivered me safe inside the ring.

And you never bit me.

Horse #20 and more

I've watched you on the race track. Once or twice I betted on you, other times I rooted from a distant stand. You were the grey one with the spots or the chocolate brown who flipped her mane. The jockeys sported neon colors on your back, patterns of oranges and blues, pinks and greens. As if you needed any more splendor when your own colors glowed as you pushed through the gates.

I think I know why, sometimes, they blind the side of your

185

vision when you are flying down the track. It isn't because they don't want you to see who's coming from behind. I think it's because with me and the whole world watching you run (and run and run and run!) we cannot stand that much beauty looking back at us. It would make us feel ashamed of ourselves. Ashamed of what we do to each other, of what we do to horses, of what we do when we really open wide and stare at our first loves and then, too suddenly, forget and turn away.

You were our first loves. Thank you for preparing me to love the human kind, not as easy as any of you.

But I'm trying.

Deborah Meltvedt is a writer and Medical Science teacher at Arthur A. Benjamin Health Professions High where she encourages students to blend both science and art in their studies and career pursuits. Deborah has been published in the American River Literary Review, Susurrus, Under the Gum Tree, the SPC Tule Review, and the Creative Non-Fiction Anthology *What I Didn't Know: True Stories of Becoming a Teacher.* Deborah lives in Sacramento, California where she enjoys running near the American River. She also loves traveling, riding horses when she can, and spending time with her writer husband, Rick and their cat, Anchovy Jack.

You can contact Deborah at deborahjean7@comcast.net.

WOLF SONG

KATHY LYNNE MARSHALL

My mother was petrified of all animals—massive dogs and slinky cats, especially, but also soft bunnies and roly-poly hamsters. If a snake slithered across her path in the garden or the tiniest mouse peered out from a kitchen cabinet, she would shriek and jump onto the tallest piece of furniture within her reach. Consequently, my younger brother, sister and I never experienced the joy of having a pet during our formative years. The sole exception was fish. We did have a toaster-sized aquarium with one orange and black striped tetra and an unattractive algae eater ... soon there was only the latter. Survival of the fittest, we were told.

I was not raised to be a card-carrying animal lover, but Snoopy dogs (Beagles), Black Labradors and Cairn Terriers are so darn cute. Even so, I rarely go out of my way to pet them and I never kiss them on the mouth, as is the habit of many dog owners . . . I know where those doggy noses have been! So it was as big a surprise to me as anyone that I would marry a man who had a 120-pound Siberian Husky.

Sultan was only a few years old when his "daddy" Ken and I began dating. Sultan was a gorgeous purebred. From top to bottom, black-to-gunmetal-to-silver-to-white fur covered his flanks. His perky triangular-shaped ears were edged in short black hairs with tufts of white inside the rim and delicate pinkish-gray fur inside. His nose was prominent and black, as was the distinguished hairline framing his wide white face. He was indeed a handsome dog.

The most striking thing about Sultan was his eyes. One was ice blue, reminiscent of the dreaded White Walkers on *Game of Thrones*. The other was the same vibrant sienna brown as Ken's.

It was Sultan's eyes that startled people as we walked him to our Sacramento neighborhood park.

"Is he a wolf?" we were constantly asked by drivers, bikers, runners, and walkers.

"No, but his breed was adapted from wolves," Ken would explain. True, the Siberian Husky is a domestic dog, normally only 60 pounds, classified as *canis lupus familiaris*. With proper training they make great sled dogs. Wolves are also classified as the *canis lupus* species, with males weighing 66 to 180 pounds. Ken felt his dog was special, more like a grey wolf than a regular domesticated dog.

Our Siberian was ever-alert to birds and squirrels, both of which would taunt him mercilessly, as they flew or scampered about the sweet gum trees in our backyard, just out of his reach. "Woof-woof!" he barked sharply, attempting to scale the tree and reach his prey. That's about the only time we heard Sultan's throaty bark. He was not a yappy dog. Thankfully.

While Ken spent a lot of time preparing his boy's meals with just the right amount of fresh meat, dry kibble, and seasoning (don't ask), I was sure Sultan would be just as happy hunting his own food, just like his wolf ancestors from Northeast Asia. More times than I like to remember, a half-chewed dead rat would greet us outside the back door. I'm pretty sure that if we had a doggy door, we would have seen many more "presents" from our furry boy inside the house.

One day, we heard loud squawks outside. "Oh no! He couldn't have, could he?" Ken and I asked each other as we raced out the front door. We did not have to look very far to see the hunter traipsing toward us, wagging his bushy tail, a live chicken still flapping in his jaws. "Drop it!" Ken ordered, which his boy did immediately, saving the fowl's life. It was hard to reprimand a dog who was merely following his genetic imprinting.

Evidently, Sultan had dug under our wooden fence into the next-door neighbor's yard, finding the colorful feathered morsel in its chicken coop. How he was able to slither his huge body under the back fence so often was a mystery to me. Four times he ended up in the dog pound. Four times we were lucky some concerned citizen called the dog catcher to remove him to safety. Even a pet neophyte like me could admit Sultan was a pretty cool dude. We came to an agreement of sorts. He left me alone and I fed, watered, and let him outside when nature called, while Ken worked 24-hour shifts with the Sacramento Fire Department. But there were limits. I was not raised with animals, so I could not stomach him being allowed on our couch and certainly not on our bed!

One of my pet peeves is heavy breathing from anyone. Now I fully realize Siberian Huskies had evolved to be sled dogs in the freezing Arctic. Our poor guy baked in the sweltering one-hundred-degree temperatures in the Central Valley. Ken would usually give his boy a buzz cut during the summer months, but it was still too hot for a snow dog. Sultan had a habit of lying on the cool linoleum floor in the kitchen, usually under foot when I was trying to fix dinner. Even though I understood he had to cool himself off somehow, the panting and dripping from his moist tongue drove me nuts!

We had a truce, the dog and me. I did not compete with him for Ken's affections nor did Sultan growl when I embraced his dad.

After a few years, we bought a house with a large yard. I had mellowed considerably and Sultan and I began to get along famously. We often played with a humongous leather chew toy. I would hold one end of the bone and Sultan would grab the other with his powerful jaws. Me shouting, "Mine! Mine!" he would growl with pleasure at our alpha game. I would lift my side of the bone up high, while he clenched his teeth around it, lifting his hefty weight off the ground. I would let him back down carefully then let go of the bone. He would run away with it and I would scamper after him, often on all fours, yelling, "Mine! Mine!" once again. He would drop the bone down the hallway, waiting for me to come and grab it, then we would start the sequence all over again. It was so much fun!

When Ken was at work, I would comb Sultan's unkempt

fur, which ticks found so alluring. Huge clumps came out in the de-matting dog comb, often with the detritus from his digging forays. I could literally fill a grocery bag with the fluff. It was meditative for both of us, sitting next to each other on the olive-green shag carpet, me detangling his shaggy mane, him dangling his pink tongue roguishly from his mouth, panting quietly, his eyes closed in pure bliss. Oddly enough, Sultan's most sensitive spot was the same as mine: on the top of the head between his ears. Scratching those nerve endings could bring us both to ecstasy.

Sultan and I had one guilty pleasure, but we only indulged in it when we were alone. I closed the windows and front screen door so nobody could hear or see us. As I got down on the floor, he would look at me and seemingly smile, his paws on my outstretched leg. I asked in a soft voice, "Do you want to sing?" He pawed my leg again. I would raise my head upward toward the ceiling as a wail started deep in my throat and rose in volume, "Owwhooooa!" exited my pursed lips. In return, my choral companion voiced the same thing: "Owwhooooa!" No matter what tone or pattern of sounds came out of my mouth—"Oww-oww-owww!"—Sultan would replicate them exactly—"Oww-oww-owww!" Sometimes he took the lead in the melody and I would follow, with the guttural resonances at the bottom of our chords reaching soprano notes at the high end of our wolf song. Our choir practice could last an hour or more until our voices were spent, raspy, and satiated. He would lay his big head on my arm and I would rub the favorite spot between his ears.

Who would have dreamed after my pet-free beginnings this wolf-dog would become my bosom companion, just like Ayla in *Clan of the Cave Bear*?

Kathy Lynne Marshall's lifelong infatuation with African culture was challenged when a DNA test revealed her diverse ancestry. Her award-winning *Finding Otho: The Search for Our Enslaved Williams Ancestors* is a part-research, part-story, part-guidebook that contains a "Solve Your Mystery" chapter, extensive research into life in Maryland, sleuthing techniques, and a DNA analysis section to help others find their ancestors. *The Ancestors Are Smiling!* contains real life stories from the descendants of Otho Williams. Both books are in the Library of Congress and research libraries across the United States. Marshall has additionally published over a dozen family history biographies. She has a short story in the upcoming *Daddy Issues* Anthology and *Wolf Song* is her first animal short story.

Her website is www.KanikaMarshall.com.

SAVING COY

L.D. MARKHAM

A s she walked along the South Rodeo Beach Trail in
Sausalito, Savannah heard what sounded like a crow's
caw followed by a moan; definitely like an animal in
distress, but saw nothing as her eyes scanned the beach. The
noise returned, and seemed more urgent.

Savannah moved toward the cove. A young seal with a coat
of silver and dark grey spots lay wedged in a kelp-draped
outcrop in a corner of the cove.

*How did you manage to get yourself into that spot little guy? Did the
tide bring you in?* As a marine biology major at U.C. Santa Cruz
and a once a week volunteer at the Marine Mammal Center not
far from where she stood, Savannah was confident the animal
was a Pacific Harbor seal. Harbor seals don't move easily along
the beach and it was unusual to find one in that particular area.

She worked her way over the outcropping of rocks with
caution to get a closer look. "Hey there, what are you doing
here?" Fortunately, no one else was on the beach, as it was
early April and still cool.

That was a good sign, no one had been around to take
selfies or bother the little guy. No other seals were in the area
and no mother seal was nearby. Savannah thought the seal was
old enough to have been weaned, but was still young.

The creature's big, round, sad-eyes looked her way. "Are
you hurt?" she asked in a soft comforting voice.

As if to answer, the seal issued another plaintive moan.

Climbing around some boulders, Savannah caught the glint
of fishing line reflecting in the sun. The line was tangled around
a flipper and the seal's neck. The animal was thin and Savannah
was concerned it was starving.

Her fingers tapped the number to the Marine Mammal Center on her smartphone and reported the distressed animal she'd quickly named Coy, because of where he was found. "I have a Pacific Harbor Seal entwined in fishing line. We're at the cove at the end of South Rodeo Beach Trail. Bring a carrier and a vet if one is available. I think it's old enough to be on its own, but it looks weak and thin. I'm the only one on the beach at the moment. I'll send you a picture." Savannah aimed her phone, and then sent the shot via text to the center.

* * *

The rescue team and vet arrived within fifteen minutes. Savannah and another volunteer held Coy down while the vet cut away the fishing line.

"The seal does have a laceration on the front right flipper, looks like the line was close to choking our friend. You're right, Savannah, he's malnourished. We'll get him back to the center and you can mix up your famous fish shakes and see if he'll take it." Dr. Phillips jotted some notes on his clipboard. "Let's get our friend into the carrier. Jim, you'll need to help Savannah."

"I named him Coy since he was alone on the rocks and seemed timid. Thought it would be easier to refer to the seal by a name. I hope that's okay?" Savannah said.

Dr. Phillips nodded.

Jim brought the carrier closer. "It may take the two of us to lift him off these rocks." Jim put on a pair of thick gloves and handed a second pair to Savannah, "Ready?"

"Yep. Let's do this."

Jim had to do most of the work since she was standing in an awkward position. They were able to get the back of the animal pushed in and the door closed.

Dr. Phillips punched numbers on his phone. "We're coming back with the harbor seal. The animal will need its own pen so we can feed and observe it for a couple of days."

He ended the call, and returned the phone to his pocket.

193

Looking at Jim and Savannah, Dr. Phillips said, "Let's get little Coy loaded onto my truck."

The two men lifted the carrier into the back of the vehicle. "I'll see you back at the center," Savannah said as she walked back to her SUV. Her heart was racing, excited about her find and anxious for the seal's fate.

* * *

Coy had stopped moaning and settled into his new digs. The center had used temporary glue to affix an ID tag to the top of his head, and Coy looked like he was sporting a miniature top hat.

Savannah had gone to the kitchen to make a special recipe fish shake containing high fat milk protein powder, fish oil, and water. Classified by the Marine Mammal Center as a Topside Animal Care Volunteer, Savannah was able to aid in the weighing and feeding of her new friend. In addition, her responsibilities would include cleaning the animal's pen and pool along with updating the patient's chart.

Coy's so cute and vulnerable. I wish I could hug him, and bring him home. This will be a great learning opportunity too. She hit the blender button and grinned.

Once the shake was finished and the patient paperwork updated, she grabbed a feeding tube, the shake, and a syringe, and headed toward Jim at the holding pen to feed Coy. *Maybe they'll let me visit and help Coy on the weekends too.*

"Hey Coy, it's dinner time." As Savannah approached, Coy was lying flat on the cement deck with his head down near the water, but not in it. "If you eat this, I promise you'll be eating fresh fish in no time." Was that a little gleam in Coy's sad round-eyes?

"Jim, I need you to position yourself at his back end and restrain him so I can get this tube into his esophagus."

Savannah gently pushed the soft, flexible tube into the animal's throat, filled the syringe with the shake formula, and pushed the syringe to deliver it.

Coy tried to move, as if he was uncomfortable, and some of the formula came back up through his mouth.

"That doesn't look good." Savannah turned to Jim with concern on her face. "I wonder if he has a blockage in his esophagus? Stay with him, I'll go get the vet."

Dr. Phillips arrived and kneeled down at Coy's side, gently rubbing his throat. "Let's get an x-ray and see what's going on. There appears to be something other than the fishing wire affecting his appetite."

The team brought Coy to the x-ray table and injected a small dose of a sedative to keep him calm. The vet's assistant took x-rays from a couple of different perspectives. As they viewed the x-rays on the screen, the doctor pointed to a light area in Coy's throat.

"Looks like he has a blockage here. It's slightly bigger than a quarter, a plastic bottle cap perhaps?" The vet rubbed his chin in contemplation. "This thing is big enough to block food, but I'm surprised it's not bothering his breathing. Prep him for surgery. Let's remove the obstruction. Get an I.V. into him with electrolytes and get him hydrated."

"Doctor Phillips, can I watch the surgery? I promise I'll stay out of the way. I'm really worried about Coy and I'd feel better if I could see you remove that obstruction," Savannah asked.

"Sure, I'll need you to stand back from where we're working, but you can see everything on the monitors. You'll need to get suited up and be sure to grab a mask. We don't want to introduce any human germs to our patient. Harbor seals can be very susceptible to people-bugs."

Savannah walked to the locker room and donned scrubs, shoe booties, facial mask and sterile gloves.

Dr. Phillips' first order was the anesthesia and use of a ventilator to help Coy breath during surgery. This was a delicate balance as seals may not breathe under anesthesia at all. The doctor inserted an endoscope down Coy's throat and turned to watch the progress of the probe on a monitor. He used long tweezer-like forceps attached to a flexible tube and a hand control much like a joy stick to gingerly remove the blockage.

After a couple of hours, the surgery was completed. The doctor successfully removed the plastic obstruction. With IV lines, a catheter, and monitoring wires, Coy was moved to a recovery room for observation.

Doctor Phillips removed his gloves and mask and looked over to Savannah. "Good call on Coy. Now we watch him overnight. If everything goes well, we'll feed him one of your famous shakes in a couple of days."

"I know I'm only scheduled one day a week, but if it's okay, I can come by on Saturdays until we release him. I'd really like to be a part of his rehabilitation."

"Are you sure? You're making a two-hour drive one day a week already." Dr. Phillips smiled as he caught Savannah's determined expression.

"I'm sure. I really enjoy working here, and I feel responsible for Coy. I'd really like to make sure he gets healthy. I don't have school then so I don't mind the drive. I know I'm not supposed to get attached to our patients, but it would make me happy to help him."

"Then that sounds like a great idea. You can try feeding him again Saturday. I'll let you write the final report; do you think your school will give you credit?"

"I don't know. I'll ask my professor. It would be a great opportunity even if they won't."

Savannah knew that Dr. Phillips was grateful for her enthusiasm and willingness to learn. It wasn't always easy to find such competent volunteers to meet the shifts required by the center.

* * *

Saturday came and Coy was looking much healthier. He was well hydrated and the night shift had given him lots of TLC. Savannah and Jim tried the feeding tube again, and this time were successful. The food stayed down.

"Dr. Phillips, the feeding tube is working. How long before we can start testing him with the frozen fish in the shallow pool?" Savannah asked.

"We'll watch him with the feeding tube for a couple of days, make sure he is gaining weight. Perhaps by your next visit you can do the test, but he's responding well. I'm hoping we'll be able to release him in another couple of weeks."

"That's great news."

By her scheduled visit on Tuesday, Savannah was able to use the pole to drag frozen fish along the water in the pool to see if Coy would respond. He passed with flying colors. The next step was to put him in the pool with other seals, fresh fish, and test his hunting abilities. The following Saturday visit, he was doing just that.

At this rate they would release him on time.

* * *

The day for release had come. Savannah was elated for Coy to get back to the ocean where he belonged, but thinking about saying goodbye to her friend was sad, and she could feel tears starting to form. She had enjoyed every minute of bringing him back to health, and was now certain marine biology was the career for her.

The release team at the Marine Mammal Center, along with Jim, Dr. Phillips, and Savannah drove to a spot just south of where Coy was found. They brought the carrier mid-beach, volunteers held up the plywood barriers to help guide Coy back to the water, and Savannah had the privilege of opening the carrier door.

Coy sniffed at the air with apprehension before deciding to move, but inched himself out of the carrier to the shore's edge. Coy turned to look back at the small group.

"Look, he's saying goodbye," Savannah said as the first tear trickled down her cheek.

Coy crept closer to the water and a wave lifted him forward. The crowd watched him for several minutes before he was out of sight.

* * *

Savannah's volunteer work at the Marine Mammal Center seemed more important now that she had become so attached to Coy. A satellite tracking tag had been attached to the seal's head with waterproof superglue prior to his release and she looked forward to checking his location every time she was at the center.

There was some relief knowing the tracker could follow him up to 2500 meters and if he seemed distressed the satellites would pinpoint his location for another rescue. The tracker would stay with Coy until either the glue failed or the seal molted.

Savannah's heart felt full nursing distressed marine mammals and returning them to their home.

Especially Coy, and on warmer days Savannah would pack a lunch and go to Rodeo Beach, eyes focused on the sea hoping to catch a glimpse of him, playing or hunting in the area.

L.D. Markham is a member of Northern California Publishers and Authors, Sisters in Crime, and the local chapter Capitol Crime, and has written several short stories. Her debut novel, *Murder in Costa Rica*, launched December 2, 2018. She is employed with the CA Department of Justice, Attorney General's office where she teaches desktop, professional development, business writing, and proofreading classes. She is also a contributor to DOJ's internal newsletter *Justice Journal*. L.D. Markham resides in Cameron Park, Ca.

Her website is www.Ldmarkhambooks.com.

WILD THINGS BELONG IN THE WILD

ANGELICA JACKSON

I first realized something was wrong when I heard a loud peeping, like an entire chicken coop on alert, coming from outside our living room. We didn't keep any chickens, so I crept up to the open window to see what was out there.

A pair of California quail, trailed by dandelion-puff chicks, dithered back and forth near our birdbath. Made from a plant saucer recessed into the gravel, the lip of the bird bath rested even with the ground, and a half dozen of the little ones must have tumbled in when the parents came to get a drink.

The hapless chicks swam along gamely, but could not climb the saucer's lip. The parents clucked their encouragement, but how long could the chicks keep paddling with waterlogged feathers?

I wavered in indecision while questions raced through my mind: Would the parents be frightened off and abandon their young if I went out to help? *Should* I help, or not interfere with nature's checks and balances? Either way could spell disaster for the little family.

I decided to at least get the chicks out of the water, and perhaps their parents could take over from there. When I opened the front door the male flew off, but the mother took her remaining chicks as far as a scraggly ceanothus bush.

At my approach, those in the birdbath redoubled their efforts to get out of the water, peeping louder all the while, but it was not enough to earn their escape. Slowly, I knelt beside the birdbath and scooped out the first chick. Even when wet, it couldn't have weighed more than a dime.

Tiny claws scrabbled against my palm and its wings

fluttered against my cupped fingers. Its legs were churning before they touched the ground, the momentum carrying it in a stumble to its waiting parent and siblings.

The next chick, and the next, behaved much the same, but the last one had faced a few more moments of panic. Wetter and weaker, this last chick struggled feebly in my hand before heaving a sigh and settling into the curve of my fingers.

For a moment I thought the stress had been too much for it, but the minute feathers on its chest still moved in and out. One dark bead of an eye turned towards me as if calmly awaiting its fate.

I felt a momentary conflict, between my naturalist training (wild things belong in the wild) and the very human impulse to make an exception for such a helpless youngster (surely the mother wouldn't miss just one). But in the end, I did not slip the bit of fluff into my pocket and carry it away. Instead, I carefully placed the chick in a sunny spot, where it keeled over on its side. Its mother called anxiously, energizing the chick enough to totter over and join the rest of its family.

Back in the house, I watched as the mother fussed over all her brood beneath the ceanothus bush. Satisfied that they were safe, she set out for the protection of our garden and the undeveloped acreage beyond.

Another crisis developed, though, when the chicks encountered the two-inch edge of the concrete driveway. More loud cheeping and scrambling over each other ensued, until the mother came back and led them to a spot where the concrete was thinner. Finally, they were all on their way.

Alas, their cries had caught the attention of other neighborhood birds, like the Cooper's hawk who swooped down and sent the mother into a panic. She froze momentarily at the threat, as if unable to decide whether she should dash back to the ceanothus or continue to the blackberry bushes on the edge of the garden. The berries offered little protection since I had recently trimmed the spent vines, but she urged her young under their spare protection.

The raptor lit on a nearby branch to study the puzzle of the espaliered vines and hurricane fence. Just as he gathered himself to fly at the little family, my human impulses won out over the naturalist training. Framed in the window, I waved my arms and cried, "Booga booga."

The hawk sheared off and returned to his oak branch, giving mother quail enough time to sprint across the gravel for the mahonia and its dense, prickly leaves. The chicks instinctively followed, but the hawk's hunting skills won out. In a dive so quick I barely had time to decide not to interfere, the Cooper's snatched up a chick and made off with it into a grove of trees.

Mother quail and the rest of her brood made it to their prickly fortress, but off in the trees the luckless chick was consumed: one, two, three bites at most. Still hungry, the hawk flew down to inspect the blackberry bushes for any other stray morsels. No sound came from the holly grape, but as the hawk turned his sharp eye that way I imitated the cheep of a little chick as a diversion.

He landed on the gravel outside the window and I stopped my noises before he could catch onto my trick. The raptor carefully peered into the ceanothus bush and stalked around the irises before flying off. I suspected that he was just biding his time nearby however, since the regular flocks of songbirds never made their afternoon appearance at our feeder.

Within a few days, the quail chicks dashed around with a lot more coordination. Their mother had a few more lessons to learn, though, since her gang of thirteen shrank to nine— and then to five. Those five soon were flying and lost their downy feathers for their grown-up colors.

Shortly after this, we elevated the birdbath so that it was less of a danger to new hatchlings. I never saw chicks that young again at the bath, but I did see quail in my garden and suspected they had chicks nearby. Those parents, with their hard-earned wisdom, chose to keep them safely hidden.

Angelica R. Jackson is a writer, artist, and avid naturalist living in the Sierra foothills of California. She is currently owned by a reformed-feral tabby cat and two adorable rescued dogs.

In 2012, she started Pens for Paws Auction, which features critiques and swag from agents and authors to raise money for a no-kill, cage-free cat sanctuary called Fat Kitty City. She is an active volunteer in the Society of Children's Book Writers and Illustrators' CA North/Central region, where she served most recently as the Illustrator Coordinator.

She is the author of the *Faerie Crossed*, young adult urban fantasy series, and her photos are collected in *Capturing The Castle: Images of Preston Castle* (2006-2016).

Made in the USA
Monee, IL
30 August 2021